fame, glory,

and other things on my to do list

fame, glory,

and other things on my to do list

JANETTE RALLISON

WALKER & COMPANY

NEW YORK

First published in the United States of America in 2005 by
Walker Publishing Company, Inc.
Distributed to the trade by Holtzbrinck Publishers

For information about permission to reproduce selections from this book, write to Permissions, Walker & Company, 104 Fifth Avenue, New York, NY 10011.

Library of Congress Cataloging-in-Publication Data available upon request
ISBN 0-8027-8991-9 (hardcover)
ISBN-13 978-0-8027-8991-4 (hardcover)

Book design by Jennifer Ann Daddio
Book composition by Coghill Composition Company

Visit Walker & Company's Web site at www.walkeryoungreaders.com

Printed in the United States of America

10 9 8 7 6 5 4 3 2 1

To the 2002 cast of
Chandler Teen Drama, whose
disastrous (but politically correct)
play was appreciated by at least one
parent. And especially to Asenath,
our drama queen, whose life keeps me
well equipped with plot ideas

one

In my opinion, children ought to be able to choose their own names. I mean, think about it. Most people wouldn't let their parents pick out their next pair of shoes, but these same parents pick out the names their offspring are stuck with for life.

Is that really fair?

I would have never chosen the name Jessica for myself. First of all, there are enough Jessicas in the world. Even though Three Forks, New Mexico, is small by anyone's standards, there are four Jessicas in my junior class. It's hard to have a sense of identity about your name when you only have a quarter ownership in it.

Second, when I graduate, I want to go to UCLA and major in acting. I need a Hollywood name—something that shouts, "This person is destined to put their hands in the cement outside of Grauman's Chinese Theater." Jessica sounds like the type of name you're most likely to see on the vest of a person working at Wal-Mart. Which, incidentally, is where I work after school two days a week and all day Saturday.

Mostly I stock things and direct people to the cat food, or whatever. It's all pretty boring, and while I'm working, I think about my future life of fame and glory and how one day I'll sit on the set of the *Tonight Show* and laugh about my crummy high school jobs.

"Well, Angelique," the host will say to me . . . or maybe, "Well, Cassiopeia, . . ."

When I reach stardom, I will also have hot Hollywood-babe boyfriends who drive Porsches, and I will totally not think about the fact that Brendan Peters dumped me back in my junior year of high school. At least, I will not think about him except for those times when he tries to scale the walls to my estate in attempts to see me and beg for my forgiveness. Then I will have my security guards escort him away. After all, one doesn't easily forgive a guy who dated you for an entire year and then, without two words of explanation, dumps you for some stupid cheerleader. I mean, excuse me, the only redeeming qualities Lauren Riverdale has are a good set of pom-poms.

It's been a week and a half since Brendan broke up with me, but I try not to think about him. He only crosses my mind when I see Lauren and him walking around the hallways holding hands, or when they eat lunch in the cafeteria sitting so close together you'd think they were Siamese twins, or when I cry myself to sleep every night. But besides all of that, I'm doing really well.

On the night I met Jordan, I wasn't thinking about Brendan at all. After my shift at Wal-Mart was over, I walked out into the parking lot debating the merits of boy names for girls instead of dwelling on the fact that it was Friday night and Brendan and Lauren were out somewhere practicing their Siamese twins routine.

And when you come right down to it, none of it was my fault anyway. It was my father's fault for buying a silver Honda

Civic when there are already approximately three billion silver Honda Civics clogging up streets and parking lots across America. I had a car with as much originality as my name. My Honda was the Jessica of the car world.

The whole thing was also my father's fault for not believing me that the starter motor on our Honda only worked half the time. "It always starts up fine when I drive," he told me. "You just need to be gentle with it."

Right. It's a car. You're supposed to put the key in the ignition, turn it, and—voila—the engine should work. Gentleness has nothing to do with it. Still, I took to patting the steering column sympathetically before I put the key in and saying, "There, there, be a good car."

Mostly, however, I blame my mother for the incident. She's the one who's always cautioning me about the massive criminal population who lurk around waiting for unsuspecting teenage girls to walk by so they can jump out and mug us.

I live in a city where half the population doesn't lock their doors at night, but I'm still paranoid every time I leave work after dark. Wal-Mart is in the center of downtown. The parking lot is well lit, and there are two restaurants in the same strip mall. So it's not like the place is abandoned even at nine o'clock, when I get off. Every few minutes somebody walks by.

I was only jumpy because of Mom.

I walked across the parking lot, jangling my keys like I was keeping rhythm to a song. *Sheridan*. I could see myself as a Sheridan, or maybe a Taylor. I checked among the shopping carts and parked cars. Nothing suspicious.

A quick glance over my shoulder revealed a teenage guy who had come out of Wal-Mart about a minute after me. His brown hair was pulled back in a ponytail. He wore some biker-looking leather jacket, and a couple of holes spread across the knees of his jeans. He strode across the parking lot in the same direction I was walking. Definitely a guy with "lurker" potential. I hurried to my Honda, got in, and locked the doors.

Of course, this didn't actually make me safe. The front window was halfway rolled down, and since the windows are electric, I couldn't roll it up until the car started.

I put the key in the ignition and turned it. Nothing happened.

I pulled the key out, put it back in, and patted the steering wheel. "Come on car, don't fail me now."

Nothing again. Not even the grinding sound I sometimes got when the car was being difficult.

"If you start, I promise I'll stop calling you a go-cart-with-delusions." I turned the key and got the same results. The car obviously knew I was lying.

Something moving outside my window caught my attention. I turned and saw the lurker guy standing two inches away from me, leaning down so he could look in the window.

"Ahhhhhhh!" I jumped so high my legs banged into the steering wheel and the keys tumbled from my hand into the darkness of the floor.

I stared back at him, my heart beating as quickly as I wanted the car to go. *He's just lost,* I told myself. He wants directions or something. He has a perfectly legitimate reason for leaning up against my car.

He tilted his head at me and sounded impatient. "What are you doing in there?"

I had to find the keys. Keeping my eyes on him, I reached down to the floor, feeling for them. "Do you need something?" I asked.

"Yeah, I need you to get out."

So that was it. He wasn't even going to pretend to be anything but a criminal. Forgetting the keys, I grabbed my purse from the seat next to me. It was the only thing I could use as a weapon, and I held it unsteadily in front of my chest. I could swat his arms with it if he tried to reach in and unlock the door. "Get away from the car or I'll scream!" I yelled.

He didn't move away. In fact, I'm pretty sure he rolled his eyes.

I let out a scream at the top of my lungs. Unfortunately, I was still so frightened I choked on it halfway through, which made it sound more like a poor imitation of a yodel than a cry for help.

He looked around. I looked around. We were still alone in the parking lot.

"Are you going to get out now?" he asked.

Suddenly I remembered my cell phone. I unsnapped the flap of my purse. "I'm calling the police," I told him.

He folded his arms. "Yeah, you go ahead and do that."

As I rummaged through my purse I kept glancing back up at him to make sure he didn't reach into the car to unlock the door. I memorized his features so I could give an accurate description to the police.

He was at least my age, probably older. Maybe even in his twenties. It was hard to tell since he looked like a thug in his leather jacket and ponytail. He had dark brown hair and brown eyes that stared impatiently back at me. Square jaw. Broad shoulders, at least six feet tall. He wore a single gold earring. I would have thought him attractive if I'd seen him under other circumstances—which, sitting in the car searching for my phone, was a strange realization. At any rate, I'd definitely be able to pick him out of a lineup.

My fingers sifted through lipstick tubes, old receipts, a pack of gum, loose change, an emergency tampon, and then another emergency tampon because I can never remember whether I put one in my purse or not, a half-eaten power bar, my wallet, a hair scrunchy . . .

He put one arm on the top of the car. I could hear his fingers tapping against the metal. "The number is nine-one-one," he told me.

Great, I was going to be mugged by a sarcastic criminal.

"Yeah, I know," I told him. "I'll call it as soon as I find my phone."

More tapping from his fingers.

I'd reached the bottom of my purse. The phone wasn't there. I started searching through the contents again, spilling them onto the seat in my hurry. I still didn't find it. I must have left it home sitting on the charger.

"The nine is the number that looks like an upside-down six," he said.

Sarcastic, and mocking to boot. I took a deep breath and tried to stay calm. "How about I just hand you my purse, and you go away."

"No dice. I've seen your purse, and there's nothing in it I want."

He didn't want my money. A bubble of panic caught in my throat. I screamed again, this time louder.

You'd think someone somewhere would have heard me and come out to see why I was screaming. No one did. The only effect my noise had was that the lurker guy took a step back from the car. While he did, I bent over, feeling along the bottom of the car until I found my keys. Fumbling with them a second, I took the Honda key and jammed it into the ignition. I wrenched it forward without any thoughts of gentleness.

Nothing.

I tried again, this time turning the key so hard it cut into my finger.

Still nothing.

The lurker guy bent over toward me, putting his hand on the top of the driver's side window. With my purse I smacked at his fingers, spilling pencils, receipts, and loose change everywhere. And all the while I pumped the key with my other hand.

"Ow!" he yelled at me, but more with irritation than pain. He moved his hand away but tilted his head back toward the window. "Look, I don't know what your problem is, but will you please just get out of my car?"

His car—he was a carjacker. No wonder he hadn't taken my purse. He wanted my car. I tried desperately to start it a couple of more times.

If ever there was a time when I needed this stupid Honda to run, it was now—right now—but it wouldn't. I jerked the keys out of the ignition in disgust.

"You want to steal this car? Fine. Go ahead. The joke's on you because it won't run. Good luck trying to get it out of the parking lot."

He took a key chain from his jeans pocket and held it up for me to see. "Well, it usually helps if you have the right key."

I stared at his hand for a moment, not realizing what he was saying. And then I saw it—behind him and off to the left. Another silver Honda sat in the parking lot. A silver Honda that inexplicably had my license plates.

I screamed again, but not loudly. It was more like a yelp of humiliation. I looked around at the seats, still not quite believing it. For the first time I noticed a circular charm with a figure of a man in a maze hanging from the rearview mirror.

"This isn't my car!" I gasped.

"Yeah. Big surprise. Do you want to get out now?"

For another moment I sat stunned in the seat—staring at him, then at my car, then back at him. I shut my eyes, both relief and humiliation washing over me. I wasn't going to be a mugging victim tonight, just a complete idiot. "I'm so sorry," I sputtered. "It's just I have a silver Honda too. See, it's right over there, and I thought this was my car . . ." With shaking hands, I grabbed the stuff that had spilled out of my purse and shoved it back in. As I did some of my anger returned. "You know, you scared me to death. Why didn't you just tell me this wasn't my car?"

He shrugged. "I came out of the store, and some stranger was sitting in my car talking to it. What was I supposed to think?"

I slipped my purse over my shoulder, unlocked the door, and swung it open. "So you thought I was crazy?"

"Well, most people would have suspected something was wrong when their key didn't work the first time."

I stepped out of the car, glad he couldn't see me blushing in the darkness. "Yeah, but my key turned in your ignition, and besides, my car only works half of the time anyway. It doesn't like me." And then because he might think I was crazy after all, I added, "I mean, the starter motor doesn't work all of the time."

He nodded as though this made perfect sense, but I knew he just wanted to get rid of me. "No harm done," he said as he slid in. "Well, probably." Then he looked at the ignition as though I might have broken it with all of my key twisting.

"Sorry," I said again, then trudged over to my car, my keys still in my hand and my purse thunking against my side the whole way.

Stupid car.

Stupid lighting.

Stupid guys who think you're crazy instead of calmly informing you that you're sitting in the wrong car.

I yanked open my car door, dropped onto the front seat, and tossed my purse down beside me. I shoved my keys into the ignition, and turned them. The car mumbled a weak grinding noise in return.

I turned the keys again. More grinding.

Not again.

Not now when I really, really wanted to go home and forget this evening ever happened.

"Don't do this to me, you horrible car," I said, and not gently.

I tried the ignition again. And again. A pathetic clicking noise replaced the grinding noise.

For the fourth time that night, I screamed—although really softly, since I figured with my lousy luck someone would actually hear me this time, call the police, and then I'd have to explain why I was sitting alone in my car screaming.

I leaned back in my seat and reviewed what, if any, options I had that didn't involve screaming—although technically speaking, everything I thought of involved screaming at my father when I got home for not fixing the car in the first place.

The other silver Honda pulled up next to mine, and the lurker guy rolled down his window. "Car problems?" he asked.

I nodded back at him limply. "The starter motor. Apparently it's gone from working half the time to working none of the time."

He draped his arm out the window. "Do you need a ride home?"

It was obvious I did, and really nice of him to offer, considering a few minutes ago I'd been smacking his hands with my purse and threatening to call 911 on him.

"Thanks, but I'll just walk back into Wal-Mart and call my parents." I shrugged and smiled, hoping he wouldn't be offended. "My mom would totally freak if I got a ride home from a stranger. You know how parents are."

"Yeah, I know." He cut his engine, and then reached for something in his car. A moment later he held a cell phone out of his window. "Here— I'll save you the walk back to the store."

I reached for the phone, stretching my arm out as far as it could go, but it wasn't enough. He leaned farther out his window to help me, and the phone brushed up against my fingertips.

"Got it?" he asked.

"Just about." And then I did have it—that is, it was in my fingers for a good two seconds before it slipped out of my hand. The crash sounded very much like plastic cracking against pavement.

Which is when I realized I was not just an idiot, I was a complete jerk because this guy tried to help me and I'd probably broken his phone. "I'm so sorry." I flung open my car door, trying to find his phone on the pavement and praying I wouldn't have to give it back to him in pieces. The darkness made it hard to see anything, and I bent over and peered underneath my car.

I saw nothing but a few rocks and indistinguishable litter.

His car door opened, then shut, and he joined me in my search. A second later he said, "I found it."

I straightened up. "Is it broken?"

With a flick of his wrist, he flipped open his phone. "Doesn't appear to be."

He handed me the phone, and I held on to it firmly. I was

not going to drop it this time. "Sorry," I said again. My hands shook as I punched in my phone number. With the phone to my ear, I studied the lurker guy out of the corner of my eye— only I couldn't think of him as a lurker anymore, since in our brief encounter it turned out he'd been the normal one and I'd been the deranged lunatic.

He leaned against his car with his arms folded, and watched me.

After a minute my little sister, Nicki, answered.

"Can I talk to Dad?" I asked.

"He's not here."

"Can I talk to Mom, then?"

"Not here either."

"Well, where is everyone?"

"*I'm* here," Nicki huffed. She's fourteen and gets huffy easily.

"Yeah, but you can't drive. Where are Mom and Dad?"

"They're out grocery shopping. How come you need someone who drives?"

"Because my car won't start. When will they be home?"

"I don't know. Soon, I guess." She didn't sound overly concerned.

"Well, as soon as they get home, have them come pick me up, okay? I'm in the Wal-Mart parking lot."

"Okay," she said, but I could hear the sounds of the TV in the background and wasn't sure if she was listening to me anymore.

"Remember to tell them as soon as they walk in the door," I said.

"I'll remember," she said, huffy again. Like I didn't know there was a fifty-fifty chance this conversation wouldn't cross her mind again until breakfast time tomorrow.

I told her good-bye, and then handed the phone back to the not-a-lurker guy.

He slipped the phone into his jacket pocket. "Is someone coming to pick you up?"

"Eventually. My parents are out, but I left a message with my sister."

"Really, it wouldn't be a problem for me to take you home." He looked beyond me, out across the parking lot and into the distance. "This is Three Forks. How far away could you live—five minutes?" He said the last part scornfully, like there was something wrong with living five minutes away from where you work.

"It's six minutes," I told him. "And what's wrong with that?"

He held a hand out as though it should be obvious. "It's such a small town."

"So?"

He shrugged and put his hands in his pockets. "Forget I mentioned it. Do you want a ride home or not?"

I did and I didn't, so I changed the subject. "You're not from here, are you?"

"Nope."

Despite the fact that he was young and good-looking, I took this as the first good news of the evening. He didn't live here. I would not run into him and be repeatedly reminded that I tried to drive off in his Honda. No one would ever know about this event.

"You're just passing through Three Forks?" I asked.

"Nope."

"Visiting?"

"I wish. My mom and I moved here yesterday."

"Oh." I tried not to let my disappointment show. I mean,

just because he'd moved here didn't mean I'd ever see him again. He probably already graduated from high school and came between college semesters to help his mom adjust to a new place or something. "How old are you?" I asked.

"Seventeen."

"Crap." This was probably not the best word to use to hide my disappointment. Still, I couldn't help myself. I leaned back against my car door and ran a hand through my hair.

He raised an eyebrow at me. "Crap?"

"You're going to go to high school with me."

"Is there a problem with that?"

I folded my arms close to my body in an attempt to warm myself even though Three Forks is in the desert area of New Mexico so it never gets that cold outside. "Yeah. The problem is you're going to become the new cool-kid, which means I'm going to become the idiot who has to avoid you until you graduate because I accused you of trying to carjack your own car."

He smiled, dimples forming in his cheeks. "It's pretty funny when you think about it."

"I've been thinking about it since it happened, and it's yet to be funny."

He laughed then, which just goes to show he's not the sympathetic type.

"Do you know your class schedule already?" I asked him. "The sooner I can plan my route to avoid you in the hallways, the better."

Still smiling, he shook his head. "I haven't even started my first day of school and girls are already avoiding me. It figures."

Right. As if he didn't know he was good-looking and every other girl at Three Forks High would be throwing herself at him. "You don't know my name," I told him. "And it's dark out. Maybe if I dye my hair brown, you won't recognize me at school."

"Nah, I'll recognize you. You'd better just get it over with and tell me your name."

I kept my face totally straight. "Lauren Riverdale. And when you relate this story to everyone, be sure not to leave out the parts that make me look really stupid."

He tipped his head to one side. "That's not your name."

He was either very perceptive or my acting skills needed work. "All right, maybe it's not. But the school could use some more good Lauren Riverdale stories, so why don't we just pretend she's here and you've never seen me before."

"I can't believe you're refusing to tell me your name. The car mix-up could have happened to anyone. You shouldn't be embarrassed." The corner of his mouth turned up, and then a small laugh crept out. "Although the way you dumped stuff out of your purse trying to find your phone *was* kind of funny."

"Thanks," I said. "I feel so much better now. You've probably never had anything embarrassing happen to you in your entire life, have you?"

"Not true," he said.

"What? Did you accidentally walk into the wrong restroom once? Everyone's done that."

"I haven't," he said.

"Then what? You were talking about how much you liked somebody, and then that somebody walked by and heard you. Everyone's done that too."

He shook his head. "Not me."

"Okay, what then? One time in PE you meant to take off your sweat bottoms and you took off your shorts along with them?"

His eyebrow rose. "You've done that too?"

I blushed, and didn't answer.

"Man, you really need to start paying attention better. You're just one big accident waiting to happen, aren't you?"

"I'm not—I mean . . ." I pushed strands of hair out of my face and tried to make sense of my words. "Okay, maybe I *am* accident prone, or embarrassment prone, or whatever it is you call people who sometimes run into walls when they're talking to their friends in the hallway. But the point is, I'd really appreciate it if you didn't tell everyone about this little mishap." Still leaning against my car, I fiddled with the door handle. "Please?"

He surveyed me, then he looked from my car to his and nodded as though silently deciding something.

"Can I see your Honda for a minute?"

"My Honda?" I asked, then shrugged. "I guess so."

He opened my car door, slid behind the wheel, and inserted his key into the ignition. It turned but didn't start.

I leaned up against my car. "That's not supposed to happen, is it? Your key isn't supposed to turn in someone else's ignition."

He held his hand out to me. "Let me see your car key."

I dug through my purse for my key chain and put it in his hand.

He took out his own key and placed it against mine. "It's the same key." Smiling, he held the two up for me to see. "The makers reuse the same key codes in different states. We've got the same key."

"Then how come my key didn't start your car?"

"Because each key also has an individual microchip that only starts your own car." He handed me back my key chain. "I think we could reach an agreement about me keeping this incident quiet. You do me a favor, and I'll do you one."

I folded my arms. "What kind of favor?"

"Not a big favor, just this: You let me borrow your car sometime."

I laughed, then saw he was serious. "My car is exactly like yours. Why would you want to borrow it?"

"Part of the agreement is I don't tell you why I want to borrow your car, and you can't tell anyone about it."

I tilted my head at him, trying to discern his intent from his facial expression. "No, really. How come you'd want two identical silver cars?"

He grinned back at me. "Do we have a deal, or do I have a really good story to tell on my first day of school?"

"But how do I know you're not looking for a getaway car or something?"

He grunted and rolled his eyes. "You're determined to think of me as some sort of criminal, aren't you?"

"No . . . ," I stammered. "It's just an odd request." See, this is what happens when you listen to your mother tell you mugging stories for years. You automatically think the worst of strangers. Only, I didn't want to think the worst about him anymore. "Fine. You can borrow my car anytime you want. You know, assuming it's running."

It was then that headlights came toward us. For one moment I thought someone would ram into our cars, and then the next moment I realized it was just my dad pulling up next to my car in his truck. His door swung open, and he strode toward me dressed in his usual cowboy boots and bolo tie. Dad routinely dresses like some sort of ranch hand even though he's a junior high math teacher. "You're having trouble with your car?" he asked me.

"It's the starter motor again," I said, "Well, either that or the car is possessed by demons."

Dad opened my front door and slid halfway onto the seat,

then motioned for me to hand him my keys. After I did, the not-a-lurker-but-a-cute-guy-who-for-some-inexplicable-reason-wanted-to-borrow-my-car turned to me. "Well, I guess you're going to make it home. See you at school, Jessica."

He opened his car door while I stared at him openmouthed. "How did you know my name?"

Smiling, he sat down behind the wheel of his car. "It's on your name tag."

My hand flew to my Wal-Mart vest and the name tag pinned there. I had forgotten about it, and now felt extra-stupid for refusing to tell him my name.

"I'm Jordan," he said.

"I think the battery is dead," my dad called to me. "Get the jumper cables out of your trunk, and we'll see if that does the trick."

I turned toward my trunk, then realized I ought to tell Jordan thanks, or sorry, or at least nice to meet you; but when I turned back, he had already pulled away.

two

As it turned out, my battery was dead. Dad thought it was very considerate of the car to die right in front of a Wal-Mart, where they sell both jumper cables and batteries, you know, just in case someone needs them. While he jumped my car, he told me in this patronizing tone that eventually I'll live on my own and I'll need to learn simple car maintenance like changing tires, checking the oil, and noticing that when none of the lights in my car come on, it means the battery doesn't work.

This, he told me, is a dead give-away that I need to do something other than lean against the hood of my car and flirt with passing boys.

"You had jumper cables in your trunk and a guy who looked capable of helping you, and instead you sat around in a dark parking lot chatting." He shook his head slowly. "This is what's wrong with today's teenagers."

Um, right. I had just tried to drive away in a stranger's car. Even if I *had* noticed the minor detail of the interior lights not coming on in my own vehicle, I wouldn't have attempted to attach wires to my battery. In my flustered state I would have most likely electrocuted myself and everyone within a half a mile radius.

See, parents should think about these things before they accuse you of being irresponsible.

Anyway, without telling my dad about the first part of my parking lot adventure, I tried to explain to him that since the starter motor gives me so many problems, I hadn't thought about the battery. So then he gave me his you-just-need-to-be-gentle-with-it speech again. Like turning a key in the ignition is some art form I hadn't perfected yet. He was just too cheap to take the stupid car into the shop.

I really hoped that after he attached the jumper cables, the car still wouldn't start up, because this would prove my point—but no, the car hates me, and it purred to life as soon as Dad put the key in. While I drove home I gave the car a piece of my mind. "I'm going to let that new guy borrow you," I told it. "He'll probably use you to run over mailboxes or something, and I won't even care."

Saturday is chore day at our house, which means I try to sleep in as long as possible. Usually I can make it until ten before Mom comes bursting into my room demanding that I clean the bathroom. Of course, I used to have a good reason to sleep in until ten. I used to stay out late with Brendan on Friday night.

I woke up at 8:47, couldn't go back to sleep, so I lay on my bed wondering if Brendan and Lauren had gone out with his friends last night, and if they were all nice to her now, like they used to be with me.

Which is enough to ruin your Saturday morning even before you have to scrub out toilets.

Brendan wouldn't be happy with Lauren for long. I knew this because I knew him. Granted, he's on the football team, so maybe it's a status symbol or unwritten law or something for him to date a cheerleader; but Lauren only talks about herself, her clothes, and what shade of auburn highlight is currently in. It won't take long before Brendan's eyes start glazing over at the mere mention of shoe sales and frosty lip gloss.

Lauren thinks she is some sort of fashion diva, but excuse me, a real fashion diva would never consent to wearing a miniskirt that's purple and bright yellow, even if it *is* the cheerleading uniform.

Our school colors are actually purple and gold—colors which go together—but the athletic uniforms, the flag, and just about all other school memorabilia come in purple and yellow. Yellow is not the same color as gold, but whoever orders stuff for our school apparently thinks we won't notice the difference.

This is probably the reason our teams always lose. I mean, how can you psych out the other team when you're dressed as if Barney the dinosaur and Big Bird got together to create your uniform?

No one who knew or cared anything about fashion would wear our cheerleading outfit, so I don't know why Lauren thinks she's the "supersized" version of cool. And I certainly don't know why Brendan agrees with her.

Besides, cheerleading is a useless skill, as opposed to acting, which I could use to—say—steal Brendan back. And I was going to steal Brendan back. I just wasn't exactly sure how to go about it.

While I poured milk on a bowl of cornflakes the phone

rang. I stabbed my cereal with the edge of my spoon and didn't get it. It wouldn't be for me.

Nicki, who sat next to me pouring way more sugar than was healthy onto her Cheerios, plodded over to the phone. She answered it with a "Yeah, hello?" then walked back and held out the phone to me. "It's for you."

"Who is it?"

She shrugged like this was a ridiculous question. "I don't know. Some guy."

I dropped my spoon onto the table and wiped my hand against my nightgown. "Is it Brendan?" I mouthed.

"How should I know?" she said back, and put the phone in my hands.

But who else could it be? No other guys had shown any interest in me since Brendan dumped me.

For a moment I just looked at the phone. *Let it be him. And let it be him for some good reason, and not some painful one, like he can't find his history book and is wondering if he left it over at my house.* I took a deep breath and held the phone to my ear. "Hello?"

"Hi, is this Jessica?" It wasn't Brendan's voice. My stomach felt like it physically dropped to my knees.

"Yes," I said.

"This is Jordan. The guy from the parking lot last night."

"Oh, hi." And then a moment later, when it had all sunk in, I asked, "How did you know my phone number?"

"You used my phone to call your house last night. I just looked it up on the call history."

"Oh, right. I'd forgotten about that. I mean, the phone call—not the call history part, because I do know how to work a cell phone." This is the problem with making a fool of yourself in front of someone. You become so eager not to let it happen again, you sabotage your own efforts to appear competent. I licked my lips and tried to think of something to say that would make me sound like a coherent human being. "So, how are you?" I came up with.

"Fine. I'm calling because I figured you'd know where the nearest mall is."

I picked up my spoon and stirred my cornflakes while I talked. "It's a half an hour drive away in Las Cruces, but you can find most things you need in the Wal-Mart in town. What are you looking for?"

"Clothes. But I refuse to wear anything bought at Wal-Mart."

I leaned back in my chair and gave up on my cereal. "Oh, you're a fashion elitist. I should have figured that out from those holey jeans you wore last night. I guess it's a half an hour drive for you then."

"Hey, I'd been unpacking all day. Those were my unpacking jeans. Most of my clothes—well at least some of them—are hole free. I have great clothes."

"Then why do you need new ones?"

There was a pause on the line, and then he said, "My mom's been bugging me to change my style, so we've come to an agreement. The ponytail stays if I get new clothes."

"What about the earring?"

"Mom says the earring can't go to school."

"Good, because the guys at my high school don't wear earrings."

He let out a sigh. "Yeah, I figured as much. It's always a sign you don't fit in when a girl sees you and her first thought is that you're trying to mug her."

I blushed, and was glad he couldn't see me. "Hey, it was dark, I was alone, and you didn't tell me why you were standing outside of my car. Under normal circumstances you wouldn't frighten me at all."

"Oh, well in that case do you want to go to the mall with me? Maybe you can help me pick out the kind of clothes you wear here." He let out another sigh, as though he really didn't want to give up his jeans with the holes.

I couldn't say no. Not when I'd just told him I didn't think of him as a thug. Besides, I wanted to go, which was odd since I'd started out this phone conversation being all depressed because he wasn't Brendan.

"Sure, I'll go. Do you want to take your car or mine?"

He laughed as though I'd told a joke. "I don't think I'm ready to borrow your car yet. Let's take mine."

My mood picked up considerably after I hung up with Jordan. *See,* I wanted to say to Brendan, *this proves I'm still a totally together teen princess. I've already got another date.* I ignored the fact that Jordan had called me because I was the only one he knew in town, and he only wanted to go to the mall because he was afraid the girls at school would think he was a hoodlum—which was kind of my fault too, since I'd been the one accusing him of hoodlum-ness in the parking lot last night. But hey, he'd still asked me to go with him, so it counted as a date.

Jordan picked me up at half past twelve, although we didn't actually get out the door until one, after he'd met my mom and answered all of her questions. She pretended to be all friendly by asking him where he'd moved from (California), what house he'd moved into (one in Three Forks' most elite neighborhood), whether his parents needed any help unpacking (his parents were divorced, but no, his mom had it under control), and what his mom was doing here in town. (She worked via the Internet as a freelance editor, so she could live anywhere she wanted. She chose Three Forks because her grandparents had lived here, and she'd visited their cabin up in Ruidoso every summer when she was a child. She'd just inherited the cabin and was turning it into a rental property.) I knew Mom wasn't just making polite conversation but amassing enough information on Jordan to make sure he wasn't some aspiring serial killer.

When she was finally satisfied that letting me go with him would in no way endanger my life, we walked outside. Our cars stood side by side in the driveway, looking like auto twins. I pointed to them. "See anyone could have gotten into the wrong car."

He smiled as we walked to his. "I know. Never once have I criticized you for getting into the wrong car."

I slid into the front seat, feeling an odd sort of déjà vu. Even the upholstery felt the same. Only the circular charm hanging from the rearview mirror told the difference. After I'd buckled my seat belt, I ran a finger over the charm. "What's this?"

"The symbol of the Pima tribe. My dad's half Pima."

Well that explained the dark brown hair. In one moment he went from cute new guy to *exotic* cute new guy.

As we drove through town toward the highway I played unofficial tour guide. "There's the library and the post office. Applebee's is across that street by the IHOP. IHOP is the only thing open late besides the Taco Time. That's the feed and tackle store, but just because we have a feed and tackle store doesn't mean we're a bunch of hicks."

"Right," he said. I could tell he didn't believe me.

"Where in California are you from?"

"Los Angeles."

Relaxing against the headrest, I let out a sigh. "Really? I want to live in Los Angeles."

He didn't take his gaze from the road. "You and me both."

"Seriously, I want to go there after high school and become an actress."

Now his head swung around, and he stared at me. "Man, I thought it was just people in L.A. who were delusional that way. Now the first person I meet in New Mexico wants to break into the business." He shook his head and looked back at the road. "Isn't there anybody left in the nation who wants a normal job?"

I straightened in my seat. "What's wrong with acting?"

"It's people pretending to have somebody else's life."

"So?"

He let out a grunt of disbelief.

"It's art," I insisted.

"Yeah, and ninety-nine percent of the actors I know are waiters and shoe salesmen. They're just throwing away time waiting for a break that will never happen."

I turned in my seat to get a better view of his face. "What about the other one percent?"

More head shaking on Jordan's part. "I can't believe I'm having this conversation already."

"What conversation?"

"The conversation in which I immediately transform from a normal person into a sideshow attraction. Can we talk about something else?"

I tilted my head at him. "I'm not even sure what we were talking about to begin with. What do you mean 'a sideshow attraction'?"

"Just forget about it." He pulled onto the highway, a long stretch of road surrounded by mesquite and scrub brush.

"Look, why don't you tell me about yourself? What do you do when you're not getting into strangers' cars?"

Which meant he wasn't going to tell me anything. I folded my arms. "Well, getting into strangers' cars takes up a lot of my time. I think I have Hondas down, so I'm about ready to work my way up to Saturns. But besides that, I work at Wal-Mart, do homework, and participate in fund-raisers in an attempt to keep the drama club afloat. That's sort of a touch-and-go venture. Mrs. Shale says if we can't raise money for new sets, we'll have to put on a reader's theater this fall. Like, hello, who'd want to sit through that? That's not acting . . . it's an audiotape with real people."

He stared straight ahead, and didn't say anything.

"So if you're in need of a magazine subscription or wrapping paper, I'm your woman."

Still nothing. I began to think some of my mother's views on strangers were justified. I mean, okay, so Jordan was good-looking, but this would turn into one awkward car trip if he refused to say anything for the rest of the way. I stared out the window and watched as a mile marker flashed by.

"Is it just the fame?" he asked.

"What?"

"Is that why you want to be an actress? You want your face on the cover of *People* magazine and have screaming fans snap your picture?"

"No," I said, and didn't mention my plans to gloat at Lauren and all her cheerleading friends during my Oscar acceptance speech. That sounded shallow.

"Because it isn't all glamorous," Jordan said. "You've got to worry about paparazzi, stalkers, and people asking for your autograph in the grocery store checkout line. Fans feel like they know you, so they have no problem walking up and telling you their opinion on every movie or episode you've ever shot. You have no privacy."

He sounded like he spoke from experience, and I stared at him, examining every feature as though I might suddenly recognize him from a sitcom or something. "How do you know all of this?"

More silence. Jordan tapped his thumb against the steering wheel. Finally he said, "I know people will find out sooner or later, but I really hoped it would be later. I want to get to know everyone before they all categorize me." He turned to face me, his eyes intent. "You've got to promise you're not going to tell anybody this. I mean, I haven't even started school yet."

I shrugged. "Okay. I promise."

"My dad is Christopher Hunter."

My first reaction was disbelief. I mean, it just didn't seem possible that I was riding in a car with the son of a movie star. That sort of thing didn't happen in Three Forks. But even as my lips formed the words "No way!" I realized how much he looked like Christopher Hunter. Same dark hair and eyes, same prominent cheekbones and square jaw. Christopher Hunter was part American Indian, and a Pima charm hung in front of my face.

"Very cool," I said.

He shook his head. "Well, I guess that depends on your definition of *cool*. If you mean having to act like some sort of fugitive to avoid reporters when you spend time with your father, then yeah, it's real cool."

"Sorry, I guess I hadn't thought about that part of it." I twisted in my seat to get a better view of Jordan. "Do you see your dad often?"

Jordan looked out at the road. "Not as often as I'd like. And now that my mom has moved us to Three Forks, he's got to fly down to see me. He's planning on coming here the day after Thanksgiving, I'm going to California for Christmas and spring break, and that's about all I'll see him this year."

Christopher Hunter was coming to Three Forks for Thanksgiving. I repressed my immediate desire to squeal like a four-year-old. I mean, here Jordan was confiding in me, sharing how he felt about not seeing his father, and all I could think about was meeting a movie star. Would it be bad form to ask for an autograph? Would it be tacky if I asked who his agent was?

I tried to hide my excitement, forcing my voice to stay casual. "Why can't he come down more than that?"

"I don't know. He says he's trying to get some projects going, but my dad has said that for a while. He hasn't done a movie in three years. I think he just doesn't want to get in my mom's way."

Until Jordan pointed it out, I hadn't realized that his dad hadn't been in any movies recently. For a while he'd been in every action flick to come through town. There had also been a police series called *You Can't Hide*. I watched the reruns of it faithfully when I was thirteen. Christopher Hunter had been totally hot on the TV show, and I'd taken a distinct interest in crime fighting for an hour every night.

If real police officers were that good-looking, women would go out and commit crimes just so they could turn themselves in.

"Don't your parents get along?" I asked, but my mind wasn't on the question at all. It was running mental calculations that would have impressed my math teacher. You see, there are few times in life when your prayers are answered in the way you expect. There are even fewer times when God drops down gifts from heaven that are better than anything you imagined. I'd been praying the drama club would run into a string of wealthy residents who all desperately needed wrapping paper. Instead, Christopher Hunter's son had moved to town.

I owed God for this.

Sometime in the future when I became fabulously wealthy, I would remember this moment and build a church, a homeless shelter, and a hospital wing all in an attempt to repay him.

The Drama Club was putting on the fall play at the end of October. Somehow Christopher Hunter had to see it. God didn't drop gifts from heaven unless he intended you to catch them. Christopher Hunter would see me in the play, recognize I had the talent to make it in the business, and introduce me to the right people. I'd skip along the road to being discovered—that is, if I could work out a few details like making sure the Drama Club had the money for sets, making sure Mr. Hunter came to Three Forks in October, and making sure Jordan took him to the play.

"Kind of," Jordan said. "It's sort of weird between them."

I looked back at Jordan with an interested expression, even though I'd forgotten what we were talking about. "Weird how?"

He shrugged. "It's hard to explain."

"Try," I said. "I'll understand." And if I didn't understand, at least I would remember what we were talking about.

He gave me a considering gaze. "You hardly know me. You don't really want to hear about my parents' relationship, or why it's weird."

His parents. That's right. He'd been telling me his dad didn't visit because he didn't want to get in his mom's way. "You don't have to tell me about your family if you don't want to." I ran my hand across the dashboard and pretended none of it mattered. "Last night when we talked, you never did fess up to what your most embarrassing moment was. You can tell me about that instead."

Jordan looked straight ahead, not at me. "Okay, so my mom and dad got married young. Right out of high school in fact. She had me, then worked part-time as a grocery store clerk while he worked as a plumber's assistant in an attempt to pay the bills and make it through college."

Folding my arms, I sat back against the seat. "You don't want to tell me your most embarrassing moment? How bad could it be?"

"Dad took some acting classes in college, and the rest is history. He landed a part in a soap opera before he even graduated. After his character was killed off by a psychotic woman who was actually trying to murder his twin brother's illegitimate child, he did the police show and then the movies."

"You not only know my most embarrassing moment, you were directly involved in it. It's only fair that I know your worst moment too."

"Unfortunately, Mom got tired of seeing Dad only on TV, and not much in person. It caused a lot of fights. Finally he left, and for a while neither of us saw much of him except on the cover of the tabloids. He was always heading off to France with some sitcom babe or supermodel."

"Well, okay, I can see how that would be weird."

"That's not the weird part. The weird part is that my parents aren't together."

I shook my head. "No, that doesn't really seem all that strange to me. I can understand why they're not together."

He held out one hand as though trying to show me something. "Have you ever known two people who just seem right for each other? They have the same interests, the same sense of humor—they even like the same food?"

Yes, I knew those people. Brendan and me. His friends used to laugh at us because we both liked Canadian bacon and pineapple pizza better than pepperoni and sausage. I nodded at Jordan dejectedly.

"Well, that's my mom and dad. Neither of them ever got serious about someone else, and I think it's because they can't find anyone who suits them as well as they suit each other."

Even though I'd never met her, I immediately took Jordan's mom's side in the matter. "What about the sitcom babes and supermodels? Your dad apparently found quite a few people who suited him better."

"That was all just an ego trip for my father. He was really a jerk for a while there, and I barely spoke to him for five years because of it. But the thing is, he's changed. I'm not sure my mom sees it though. I don't think either of them do."

Jordan sounded so casual about it, but I felt a stab of sympathy for his mom. I wondered if she'd ever woken up in the morning thinking of ways to win her ex-husband back.

Jordan took his glance away from the road long enough to meet my eyes. "And I know what you're going to say next. You're going to tell me that all kids of divorce want their parents back together, and I shouldn't set myself up for disappointment trying to hook them up again, because it will never happen. All my friends in California said the same thing."

He turned back to the road, as though the matter were closed.

I tapped my finger against the armrest. "I wasn't going to say that at all." My mental calculations clicked through the possibilities of the situation. "I mean, if they're really right for one another, why shouldn't you try to get them back together?

Maybe you should encourage your dad to visit you down here more, then he'd have to spend time with your mom."

"I've already tried. He's pretty firm on the not-until-Thanksgiving plan. Three Forks isn't exactly his scene. He's not really a tackle and feed store type of guy."

Thanksgiving? Too late. The costumes would be back in storage by then, and my magnificent performance all but forgotten.

Jordan gave me a grin. "But I do have plans for them when he comes up. They honeymooned in Mom's grandparent's cabin, and one way or another I'm going to get the two of them to spend some time back there."

"Oh, well, at least that's good."

It wasn't good, but I didn't know how to change it to a sooner date. For the rest of the car trip, I worried more about Jordan's mother's love life than I did about my own. Jordan and I talked about all sorts of things, but all the while, in the back of my mind I wondered how to get his father to Three Forks earlier.

When we finally got to the mall, I gave Jordan the grand tour of the best stores. Jordan outright refused to look at anything in Sears. I tried to explain to him that the clothes didn't have PURCHASED AT SEARS stamped anywhere on them, so nobody would know where he bought his clothes. But no, he told me it was a matter of principle. He couldn't buy clothing at a store that also sold dishwashers and wrenches.

Like that made any sense.

He decided Dillards was an acceptable store, where the employees wouldn't get confused and try to sell him drill bits along with his jeans, so we went there. I sifted through the racks and handed him things to try on.

At first he took the clothes skeptically—because after all I worked in Wal-Mart and had tried to lure him into Sears.

"It's not where you shop," I told him as I handed him a sweater. "It's knowing what styles are in and being able to put different things together to achieve the right look." I added a shirt to his pile. "Trust me, I know guys clothes. I used to dress my ex-boyfriend all of the time."

Over the stack of clothes, Jordan raised an eyebrow at me.

"I mean, I picked out clothes for him. At the store. Like I'm doing for you now." I blushed despite myself. "See, that's one more event to add to my list of embarrassing moments." With a flourish I pointed him toward the dressing room. "Try everything on, and I'll let you know what colors are best on you. I'm guessing green right now, but it's hard to tell."

He folded the shirts over one arm. "I just want to buy the clothes I like. I don't care about the color."

I took a shirt from a nearby rack and held it up against his chest. "Maybe blue . . . here, take this shirt too."

He took the stack to the dressing room, then every few minutes stepped out with a resigned expression on his face. "I look suburban."

"And that's a good thing," I told him.

I vetoed a couple of the shirts but put the rest in the "hot" pile, because Jordan made everything look good: green, blue, and—if he'd tried it—orange with chartreuse polka dots. He bought everything I had okayed without even looking at the price tags. As the clerk put the last of it into a bag he tucked his wallet back into his jeans. "Well, this should make my mom happy." The clerk handed Jordan the bag, and we wandered out of the store. "Do you have anything you want to shop for while we're here?" he asked.

"No, I can't buy stuff for myself with you around. That would ruin the whole mystique."

"Mystique? What are you talking about?"

As we walked down the hallway I gazed at the mannequins in the storefronts. "Guys aren't supposed to know where girls get their clothes. We just appear in them at school like fashion goddesses. If I bought something with you today, then every time you saw me wear it you'd think, 'Oh, that's the shirt Jessica bought at Dillards, on sale for thirteen ninety-nine.' It would ruin the whole image of the outfit."

Jordan swung the bag against his leg. "But what about my image? You just saw me buy everything."

"Yes, well, guys have very little mystique to begin with, so they don't have to worry about preserving it. It's better that girls help them pick out clothes so they match."

"I match," Jordan said. "I have mystique. I don't know about Three Forks, but California is full of well-dressed guys."

Like he could tell the difference. I considered the skirts in the window of The Limited as we walked by. "Okay, so what goes better with indigo—black or navy blue?"

He took a few steps in silence. "I could probably tell you if I knew what indigo was."

"I rest my case." We passed a music and DVD store, and as I looked at the movie posters hanging in the store I thought of Jordan's parents again. "Now, about getting your dad to visit your mom—have you ever considered pretending to have a serious illness? That works on TV."

"And is just one more way TV is not like real life. Doctors have diagnostic equipment that tells whether you're sick. It's not like you can fake cancer."

"How about you invite him down to do some outdoorsy guy thing then? It's almost hunting season, isn't it?"

"Neither of us hunt."

I'm not sure why this surprised me. Maybe because his last name was *hunter*. Besides, I guess I just figured anybody who spent so much time wielding a gun on TV was likely to do it in real life too. "How about camping then? That's something dads do."

"If I told him I wanted to go camping, he'd fly me out somewhere. He wouldn't come to Three Forks to do it."

We passed a jewelry store and a shoe shop, but my mind didn't let go of the problem. What could Christopher Hunter do in Three Forks, and only in Three Forks, that would require him to visit his son here?

We walked back to his car, and the conversation turned to other things; but my mind still gripped the Christopher problem, turning it around and examining all the edges. It was like being stuck on a jigsaw puzzle with only two dozen pieces left to go. I knew the right piece sat in front of me, and yet I still couldn't find it.

We climbed into his car, pulled out of the parking lot, and headed back to the highway.

"What does your dad like to do?" I asked during a lull in the conversation. "If hunting and camping won't work, something else will. What interests him?"

Jordan shrugged. "He likes to cook. He exercises a lot. I don't know. He loves acting the most."

And there it was. The piece I'd been missing. I hadn't seen it before, because it was too obvious.

I leaned back against the seat with relief. A whole quarry of birds was about to drop to the ground with just one stone from my hand. "I know how to get your dad to not only come before Thanksgiving but to stay for a while," I said.

He looked over at me skeptically. "How?"

"You're going to be in our school play. And not only do you want him to come down for the performance, you want him to come down beforehand and coach you on your part. He'd do that for you, wouldn't he?"

Jordan's eyebrows drew together. His thumb tapped against the steering wheel. "I've never liked acting. I don't know if I could do it if I tried."

"All the more reason for your father to come down and help you."

A slow smile spread across Jordan's face. "You have a point. I'd need lots of practice, and who better to help me than my dad?"

He drove silently, nodding, and I knew he was working out the details, putting the rest of the pieces together. Finally, he turned back to me. "Do you think I'll even make it past the tryouts though? What director in her right mind would choose someone who's never acted before?"

"We always need guys, and besides, I can help you. I know how to act."

And I did. For example, right now I was acting completely confident, when in reality I wasn't sure the director would choose him for anything. But somehow, I just knew it had to be.

three

Mrs. Shale, the drama teacher, says I have an expressive face. "You project emotion so well," she told me all through the production of *Oklahoma!*

It may help in the theater, but it's a pain everywhere else. I had been home from the mall for approximately five minutes before Nicki started in on me. She eyed me from her spot in the family room, where she sat perched in front of the computer. With the phone pressed against her ear, she was IMing half the freshman class. "You're in a good mood," she called as I walked into the kitchen. "Did you find some great deals at the mall?"

"Nope." I rummaged around in the fridge and pulled out a peach.

"So what happened?" she asked.

"Nothing happened." I ran the peach under the faucet, then rubbed it on a dish towel in an attempt to remove as much peach fuzz as possible.

Nicki kept staring at me. "This is the first time I've seen you happy since Brendan dumped you."

"I'm not happy."

"You're humming, smiling, and eating something that wasn't dipped in chocolate first."

Okay, there may have been some Almond Joy moments after Brendan broke up with me, and admittedly I did carry around a jumbo-sized bag of Peanut M&M's for an entire day, but that's only because I'd been stocking candy at work. When you've been looking at it all day, it's hard not to buy five or six bags.

"Maybe I am happy," I told Nicki, "but that's only because I have a naturally sunny disposition."

"Oh my gosh," Nicki said into the phone, "Jessica's in love with the guy from the parking lot."

"I'm not in love." I took a bite of the peach and juice dribbled down my chin. "And his name is Jordan."

Nicki's finger's tapped away at the keyboard while she spoke into the phone. "Yeah, I guess he's kinda cute, although I don't know what the deal with the ponytail is. I mean, that is *so* Willie Nelson. I'd never go out with a guy whose hair is longer than mine." Then to me she said, "Miranda wants to know if he kissed you."

"No, he didn't kiss me." When the surprise of the question wore off, I added, "And tell Miranda she shouldn't ask such personal questions."

"Julie wants to know if you're going out now, or whether it was a one-time deal."

I grabbed a napkin from the table and took another bite of my peach. "Just who are you talking to on the phone?"

"Priscilla. And she says if you don't want the guy, can she have dibs on him? She thinks ponytails make men look brooding."

Which meant Nicki was not only discussing Jordan and me on the telephone but also broadcasting our mall outing over the computer. I ripped the pit out of my peach, walked to the trash can, and dropped it in. "Would you please refrain

from talking about my love life with every single person you
know?"

"Too late." Her fingers tapped happily on the keyboard, and
into the phone she said, "Sounds like she wants him, Cilla. She
got all defensive when I asked if he was up for grabs."

I took my peach and stomped up to my room so I wouldn't
have to talk to her anymore. I didn't want Jordan. At least not
that way. I wanted him as a friend, and I certainly wanted his
dad as a friend; but after all, I was suffering from a broken
heart over Brendan. I wanted Brendan, and I'd even come up
with my first battle plan in the war to wrench him out of
Lauren's well-manicured hands.

It had come to me as I'd held the phone this morning—
when I'd hoped Brendan hadn't called just to tell me he'd left
his history book at my house.

I now realized that was the perfect thing for Brendan to
tell me. If he'd left his history book at my house, he'd have to
come over and get it because we had a test on Thursday and
Brendan never read the chapters ahead of time. Of course, he
hadn't left his history book at my house. It probably lay in the
bottom of his locker under empty Gatorade bottles and dis-
carded English papers. But I could steal it easily enough. He'd
given me his locker combination at the beginning of the year.

So I'd take the book Monday morning, then wait until
Wednesday to e-mail him that I'd found his book at my house.
He'd have to pick it up that night, and when he did, I'd be
waiting.

As I nibbled at my peach I planned out the details. I'd wear
my hair down and curled. He liked it best that way. I'd wear
my black angora sweater. It was feminine, pretty, and drenched
with mystique. I'd bake chocolate chip cookies so the smell
wafted throughout the house. Brendan never met a chocolate

chip cookie he could walk away from. And best of all, I'd tell him in the E-mail he needed to pick up his book before seven because I had a date after that.

Nothing is more irresistible to a guy than a girl who is dating someone else. He'd be mine again before test time on Thursday.

Which meant I could concentrate on Jordan until then, or at least concentrate on getting Jordan's acting skills up to tryout level. During our car trip home we'd arranged to meet after school on Monday to go over the script for *Romeo and Juliet*.

Mrs. Shale was such a Shakespeare fan that she occasionally spent entire class periods just waxing philosophical about the intricacies of Hamlet's character. The wall in the back of the class sported an almost life-size poster of a muscular Romeo embracing a dewy-eyed Juliet. Her long, blond, and bejeweled hair fell in loose curls around her waist. You could tell how much Mrs. Shale loved that picture by the way she'd sit at her desk and gaze at it. So I guess it was inevitable that eventually she'd try to put on the play herself.

She hadn't told us what pages she was choosing for tryouts, so I figured Jordan ought to read over the main scenes to get a feel for it. Perhaps multiple times.

I wanted the part of Juliet. In fact, I hadn't cut my hair since the beginning of sophomore year when Mrs. Shale mentioned she wanted to do the play this year. My blond hair was halfway down my back, and I'd already started practicing my dewy-eyed expression. My only real competition in the drama class, Mary East, had dark brown hair that didn't even reach her shoulders. See, now that's poor planning.

Of course, Mary's father was school superintendent, which might cancel out my long blond hair. Teachers generally bent over backward to oblige Mary, and excuse me, I don't think she got the part of Ado Annie in last year's *Oklahoma!* because of her singing voice.

Jordan, of course, would be perfect for Romeo. He was tall, dark, handsome, and the son of a famous actor. Massive genetic talent must lie beneath his surface, just waiting to be tapped into. All I had to do was help him find it within himself.

I drove to school early on Monday morning so I wouldn't have to worry about running into Brendan. I walked to his locker, spun the combination and opened the lock. After a few moments of digging around in the junk on the bottom, I walked away with his history book. It was so easy that for three or four minutes afterward, I seriously considered taking up a life of crime.

I tucked the book safely away in my locker, then looked for Jordan in case he was wandering around the hallways with his schedule, trying to find his classes. But I didn't see him, not before school and not between first and second periods. By third-period break I was looking for him so intently I nearly walked right past Lauren and Brendan without my customary gut-twisting reaction.

As they walked by holding hands, Brendan looked away, awkwardly, pretending he didn't see me. Lauren gave me a triumphant smirk. She's obviously the type of person who as a child would push the other kids off their trikes. I wouldn't even feel sorry for her after Thursday.

At lunch I saw Jordan across the cafeteria eating with a couple of the cross-country guys, so I guess it hadn't taken him long to find his niche. While I ate I pointed him out to my best friend, Kate.

I'd told her about the car mix-up, although I probably

shouldn't have. She already has this totally unjustified opinion that I'm too scatterbrained, so these types of stories do nothing to boost her confidence in me. Still, I had to tell someone, and although Kate and I are night-and-day different, she's totally loyal. I knew I could trust her to keep it a secret.

She watched him, unconcerned, over the top of her sandwich. "He's cute, but he looks kinda arrogant."

"You think all guys are arrogant, Kate."

"That's because they all are." She took a sip of her milk. "I was right about Brendan, wasn't I?"

I snapped my carrot in half. "Just because he broke up with me doesn't mean he's arrogant."

"Yeah, but I thought he was arrogant *and* untrustworthy."

It was probably useless to point out to her that she thought all guys were untrustworthy. Ever since Kate's parents divorced three years ago, she didn't have anything nice to say about the other half of the population. And you didn't want to get her started talking about pay scale, the equal rights amendment, or organized sports in general. According to Kate, football is just a way for men to vicariously act out their aggressive tendencies. And society was sick—just sick—to turn them into superstars.

I decided to steer the conversation back to Jordan. "I think Jordan would make a good Romeo, don't you?"

Kate rolled her eyes.

"I mean for the play. You know, *Romeo and Juliet.* We're putting it on in drama."

She casually took another bite of her sandwich. "Didn't you hear? Mrs. Shale decided to do a reader's theater this year."

"Only if we didn't raise enough money for sets with our next fund-raiser," I said.

Kate shook her head. "I just got out of Mrs. Shale's English class. She said she decided to do a reader's theater of *Hedda Gabler* instead of *Romeo and Juliet*."

I dropped my carrot onto the table. "No."

Kate shrugged. "You can still try out for the musical in the spring."

I couldn't wait until the spring. Anything could happen before then. For all I knew, Jordan would convince his mom to move back to L.A. before the spring.

I tilted my head back against my chair. "She's not even going to give us a chance to push magazines? How can she do this to me?"

"Look on the bright side. You won't have to memorize pages of iambic pentameter, and you can cut your hair. No offense, Jessica, but if your hair were any longer, people would think you were trying to be either a mermaid or Amish."

I bet Julia Roberts has more sympathetic friends. I bet not once did Arnold Schwarzenegger ever have to perform a reader's theater. And most importantly, I bet Christopher Hunter wouldn't fly down to see a bunch of kids sitting on a stage reading a script, even if his son was one of those doing the reading.

"I'm going to talk to Mrs. Shale after drama class," I said. "She just has to let us do a real play. She *has* to." But as I ate the rest of my lunch I felt less and less optimistic about my chances. In the history of schools, when has a teacher ever listened to what a student thinks?

I have drama sixth period. The class consists of four people who are serious about acting and two dozen who didn't want to take band, orchestra, or shop, and needed another

elective. You'd think Mrs. Shale would realize this, just concentrate on the four of us who want to act, and let everyone
else do their homework or something—but no. Every day we
all have to do exercises designed to expand our imaginations.
Like we shut our eyes, pretend to eat a lemon, and feel—
really feel—the sour, lemony taste. Today we pretended to
walk in the snow and tried to show that we felt the wind in
our hair and the cold rushing against our cheeks.

Mrs. Shale sat perched on her desk, roughly the same
shape and in the same pose as a Buddha, and waved one hand
benevolently at us. "Can you feel a shiver moving up your
spine? Can you feel waves of snowflakes brushing against
your lips?"

Next to me a guy named Andre snickered. "No," he whispered. "I just feel really stupid sitting here with my eyes shut."

Jeff and Tye, his usual partners in crime, laughed and made
noises that indicated they also felt stupid—which was probably not a new experience for them. I tried to block out this
trio, creating a blizzard in my mind to drown out their voices,
but it's hard to invent a chilling wind when you're surrounded
by unbelievers.

Mrs. Shale left her desk and walked around the room studying our faces. "Feel the frost on your fingers. Feel the sting
against your ears. Show me you feel the winter!"

Then Andre made a big production of pretending to blow
his nose on his sleeve, so that Mary and her string of friends
all burst out laughing.

"What?" Andre asked with a smile. "My nose always runs
when it's cold."

After that, Mrs. Shale assigned us an essay on *Midsummer
Night's Dream*. Thank you very much, Andre.

When class ended, I hung back, pretending to organize my books while waiting for everyone to leave.

Mary stopped by Mrs. Shale's desk to compliment her on—of all things—her black turtleneck sweater. Mary is such a suck-up. First of all, turtleneck sweaters make people look like they have no necks. When someone is overweight to begin with, and therefore short in the neck department anyway, a turtleneck is never going to be a good choice. Plus, for some reason that the student body has never been able to discern, Mrs. Shale wears almost entirely black. Theories on this range from

(a) There's a Thespian Society rule that states drama teachers must wear dreary colors.
(b) She's mourning for a lost love.
(c) She made a pact with the devil.
(d) She's color-blind, and having a completely black wardrobe makes it easier to match things.

Whatever the reason, Mrs. Shale has single-handedly put would-be Goth groupies right off the color black because anyone who wears a lot of it invites all sorts of unflattering comparisons. I mean, no one wants to hear the phrase, "Hey, you're looking a lot like Mrs. Shale today."

Anyway, after Mary had finished her attempt to secure a main part in the reader's theater through flattery, I made my way up to Mrs. Shale's desk. She shuffled through our essays and shook her head.

"Hello, Mrs. Shale, I—"

Her head cocked up when she heard my voice. "Jessica, did you read *A Midsummer Night's Dream*?"

"Yes," I stammered.

"Well, you're apparently the only one in the class who did then. The other students think it's a play about Lysol-ander, Queen Hippo, and Puke."

"Lysander, Queen Hippolyta, and Puck," I said, hoping I'd win brownie points for knowing the names off the top of my head.

"I suppose I can't blame them." She set the papers back down on the desk in a cluttered heap. "So few people can grasp the nuances of Shakespeare these days. Still, it's depressing to think that every time I give a reading assignment, there's a run on Cliff Notes somewhere."

"I love Shakespeare." I didn't, but in a class where we were routinely asked to pretend to be people who never existed, I figured it was okay to stretch the truth. "I really wanted to be in *Romeo and Juliet*—a lot of kids did. A reader's theater just won't be the same."

Mrs. Shale looked at the stack of papers and shook her head again. "I can just imagine how they've butchered the name Hermes."

"So you should expose more kids to Shakespeare. You know, help us develop an appreciation for fine writing."

She flipped through a couple of papers and sighed. "Maybe another year when money isn't so tight. I need about a thousand dollars for a set, and the school doesn't have it, because, heaven forbid, the guys on the football team would have to wear their old uniforms one more year.'"

"A thousand dollars isn't so much," I said. "I'm sure our fund-raiser would cover it." And if not, I would personally buy a lifetime supply of gift wrap to make up the difference.

Mrs. Shale patted my hand. "That's what I like about you, Jessica . . . your dedication to drama." She lowered her voice, as though telling me a secret. "No one even comes close to your rendition of eating a lemon. But we just don't have the resources." She picked up her red marking pen and turned back to her papers as though this closed the matter. On the first page she drew large, loping circles around every misspelled word.

A lump of desperation tightened in my throat. "But I know the perfect guy for Romeo."

Tonelessly, and without shifting her gaze from the stack of essays, she said, "Brendan might look the part, but I don't think he could display the inner turmoil needed for the performance."

"I don't mean Brendan. I mean Christopher Hunter's son." I actually slapped my hand over my mouth after I said this. I hadn't planned to say anything about Christopher Hunter. I had planned to say Jordan Hunter, and yet the whole Christopher Hunter's son phrase popped out instead.

Mrs. Shale's pen froze over the paper. Her glance rushed back to mine. "Christopher Hunter's son? Where would we get him?"

If I were really a good actress, I would have laughed off my mistake. I would have said, "In a drama class with Harrison Ford's and Tom Cruise's kids." But instead, I stood, hand still over my mouth, staring at Mrs. Shale. It was too late to take back my statement.

"I wasn't supposed to tell anyone," I whispered, "but he just moved here. I've already talked to him about it, and he wants to try out for the fall play. So we have to put on a fall play. I mean, Christopher Hunter will come to see it if his son is involved."

My parents wonder why I want to be an actress. If they could have seen Mrs. Shale's face at that moment, it would have answered all of their questions. Pure awe shone in her eyes.

"Well, yes," she said, letting out a low breath. "That does merit consideration, doesn't it? You say you've met him? Is he going to take my drama class? Is his father in Three Forks right now?"

"He couldn't fit your class into his schedule." Mrs. Shale didn't need to know that this was because he didn't like drama. "And his parents are divorced, so it's just his mom who's here; but his father will come down and visit if he's in the play. Maybe he could even give the cast some acting pointers. Think of what a great opportunity it would be for us kids to meet a professional actor."

"Yes," she repeated. "A great opportunity for the kids."

Only, I could tell by the faraway, dreamy look in her eyes that she was no longer thinking of the kids but of schmoozing with a handsome Hollywood hunk. You'd sort of expect more from a woman who's in her forties and married, but hey, this is the effect movie stars have on people.

"Perhaps I could talk to the principal about getting some additional funding . . ." she said, imagining herself, I'm sure, at some intimate gathering Christopher Hunter was throwing for his son's favorite teachers. Liam Neeson would no doubt be there, along with a few Rolling Stones members and a karaoke machine.

"Great," I said. "I can hardly wait for tryouts."

"Yes," she said. But I'm not exactly sure what she was saying yes to—my comment or Christopher Hunter asking her if she'd like another shrimp kebab appetizer.

"Jordan doesn't want everyone to know who he is right off, so could you keep that part a secret?"

"Yes," she said again. And I didn't even want to guess at what she was imagining.

Jordan and I met in the school library after school. We sat at a corner table by the drinking fountain with two copies of *Romeo and Juliet* propped in front of us. Mine was a thin and yellowing book containing only *Romeo and Juliet*. Jordan's was a monstrously thick copy of Shakespeare's entire works, with pages so pristine they looked like they'd never been turned. I flipped through my book until I found Romeo and Juliet's first meeting. "All right. You've sneaked into a ball being thrown by your biggest enemy, my father, and meet me, Juliet. You are at once overwhelmed by my grace and beauty."

"Yeah," he said with a smirk. "That's exactly how it was when I met you."

"Read your line, and try to show the audience you're over-whelmed." I batted my eyelashes to add to the effect.

Jordan skimmed the page till he found the right place, then read:

> *If I profane with my unworthiest hand*
> *This holy shrine, the gentle fine is this,*
> *My lips, two blushing pilgrims, ready stand*
> *To smooth that rough touch with a tender kiss.*

He laid the book down with a thud.

I picked it up and handed it back to him. "Now read it with feeling."

"Feeling? I didn't even understand what I said. How am I supposed to feel anything about it?"

Scooting my chair closer to his, I peered down at the book. "A lot of times you have to read Shakespeare two or three or a dozen times to understand what he's saying. See Romeo takes Juliet's hand and apologizes because his handshake isn't soft enough. He compares her hand to a holy shrine and says his lips are two pilgrims waiting to smooth out his rough touch with a kiss. And because he's Shakespeare and had all that prac- tice writing sonnets and stuff, he rhymed the whole thing. That's why English teachers love him." I handed his book back to Jordan. "Now try to emote while you read it."

Jordan's eyebrow rose. "He's comparing his lips to two pil- grims? That's the lamest pickup line I've ever heard."

I ignored him and read Juliet's line.

Good pilgrim, you do wrong your hand too much,
Which mannerly devotion shows in this:
For saints have hands that pilgrims' hands do touch,
And palm to palm is holy palmers' kiss.

Instead of being impressed with my reading, or at least not- ing how I'd done it, Jordan picked up his book and flipped through the pages. "I don't believe this. Does this *all* rhyme? Is any of it understandable?"

I held my hand out for the book. "Jordan, you're not pay- ing attention to the play."

"Yeah, well it's hard to pay attention to, since it makes no sense." With a flick of his wrist, he tossed the book back down on the table. "No high school student is going to pay money to watch this."

Great. I'd just convinced Mrs. Shale to try and put the play on, and now Jordan was having second thoughts. Mrs. Shale was not going to forgive me if I made her beg for more funding from the principal, and then didn't produce Jordan at tryouts. I suddenly saw my future as Juliet vanish, replaced by a future as assistant prop girl.

I picked up his book and opened it again. "The guys in the play wear tights. Trust me, girls will come see this."

He shook his head. "Two hours of listening to people speak a language that only vaguely resembles ours? Not even the girls will come."

"Why do you think we go to high school football games? We don't care which direction the ball goes. It's the shoulder pads and tight pants that get us there." I shrugged. "Besides, all the English teachers will make their classes go, as part of the Shakespeare unit."

Jordan leaned back in his chair and surveyed me through skeptical eyes. "So you're telling me the audience is made up of students who are forced to come and don't understand what's going on? I foresee a lot of audience distraction in the form of people talking during the performance, passing notes, maybe starting up a dodgeball game in the back of the room."

I held the book out to him. "Remember, you're doing this for your parents."

Letting out a sigh, he took the book from my hands and fingered the pages. "You know, faking an illness might work. Amnesia is hard to disprove, isn't it?"

"Jordan."

"This is going to be a bad play, and it will be even worse if I'm in it."

"*Romeo and Juliet* is one of the most famous plays ever written. If it were bad, someone would have noticed before now. Besides"—I waved one hand over the book as though I was brushing away his concerns—"once you get onstage, you'll see why we all love drama."

He didn't answer.

"Let's just work on the acting portion right now. I want you to act like you really like me."

He raised an eyebrow.

"You know, pretend we just met at a party, and you think I'm pretty. What do you say to me? What is your body language?"

He stared back at me in the same way Andre stares at Mrs. Shale when she asks us to pretend we're inanimate objects, like chairs or vegetables.

"Come on, Jordan, what would you say?"

He leaned forward and lowered his voice. "I can't do this. We're sitting in the library."

"No, we're not. We're in someone's living room, the music is blaring, the lights are down low, and you've just eaten half a bowl of potato chips. Now what do you say to me?"

He waved one hand at me. Slightly. "Hey." Then nothing.

I waited for more. "Hey?" I asked him.

"Hey, is there some soda around here? I'm dying of thirst after eating half a bowl of potato chips."

I grunted and tapped my fingers against the table. "Have you ever even had a girlfriend?"

"Yes, I've had a girlfriend."

"Well, you didn't use that body language to impress her."

He looked down at himself, alarmed. "What body language?"

"Exactly my point. You should look in my eyes and lean toward me with one hand draped across the table as though you want to touch me. Now, what pickup lines do you usually use when you want to date a girl?"

He put one arm across the table, but it looked more like he was challenging me to an arm wrestling match than reaching out to touch me. "I don't have pickup lines," he said. "I say whatever is on my mind. I'm a genuine type of person."

"All guys have pickup lines."

"Fine then, you tell me some. Apparently you've heard them all."

"Okay, now your body language is becoming rigid. Do you notice how you're clamping your jaws together?"

He glared at me. "No, I'm too busy gritting my teeth to notice what my jaws are doing."

"Try relaxing. Take a few cleansing breaths."

He pushed his chair away from the table and ran one hand through his hair. "There's no way I'll ever make it past tryouts."

"Yes you will. We're a small school, and we always have more guy parts than guys. It's just a matter of what part you'll get."

Besides, the drama teacher is already planning which of her black outfits she'll wear when she meets your father.

"But do you think I can get a decent part?"

"As long as we keep working on the dialogue." I tilted my head at him. "And your body language problem."

"I don't have a body language problem."

"Of course not," I said. "Now try repeating your part without clenching your fists."

He looked down at his hands, surprised, and unclenched them. "My dad makes this look so easy." He stretched out his fingers and rested them back on his jeans. After a quick glance around the library, he lowered his voice and leaned toward me. "At least no one knows who I am, so I don't have to worry about living up to everyone's expectations. That's been the only good thing about moving here. I can be me instead of the movie star's kid."

"Right," I said. Only Mrs. Shale knew about Jordan's father, and I'd told her to keep it a secret. Momentarily I considered telling Jordan I'd accidentally let his secret slip, but only momentarily.

Mrs. Shale was bound to choose him for a main role and spend lots of time fussing over how wonderful he was. I wanted Jordan to think the attention was for him, not for his father. That's what his acting really needed: a boost of confidence—a drama coach who adored him.

Still, it would be obvious to everyone, including Jordan, that something was amiss if he totally stunk at the auditions and got a huge part anyway. I had to at least get Jordan to a functional acting level. "We can work on this as long as you want to," I said. "I mean, it's good practice for me too, since I'm trying out for Juliet."

He fingered the pages of the book, then shut it. "That's all right. I'll go over it a few times by myself to see if I can get a feel for the language." Standing up, he tucked the book under his arm. "And if I can't, maybe I can convince my dad to come up for some cross-country meets. At least I know I can do those without having to speak in rhyme.

I followed Jordan up to the checkout counter, hating cross-country. I mean, what was the point of it? You ran places. How was that a valuable life skill?

As the librarian scanned his book I tried to erase thoughts of running from his mind. "Let's get together and go over the parts tomorrow after school. We can go to my house . . ." As soon as I offered the invitation I thought of Nicki IM-ing the entire freshman class with every phrase, nuance, and expression exchanged during our practice. "Or we can go to your house."

He took the book from the librarian and tucked it under

his arm. "My house is fine. Where's your locker? We can meet there first."

"I have drama class sixth period. Can you meet me there?"

Because once Mrs. Shale started fawning all over him, he'd forget all about cross-country.

Well, I hoped.

four

Kate thinks I live a charmed life. If pressed for examples to support her claim, she points out I eat whatever I want without gaining weight, my teachers all like me, and guys occasionally smile in my direction. She also brings up—like it was some sort of sign from God—the time when I was thirteen and wanted an iPod but hadn't quite saved enough money to buy one. The next day I found a fifty-dollar bill blowing down Main Street. There was no way to locate its owner. I had to keep it—or rather spend it buying an iPod. Kate still glares at my iPod as though it's treated her unfairly.

She didn't even change her charmed-life theory when Brendan dumped me. Half the girls in the junior class felt sorry for me, but not my best friend. "You're better off without him," she told me every time I let out a tormented sigh in her presence. "He's a jerk. Besides, he plays football."

Those two things, apparently, are synonymous in her mind.

She called me when I got home from school to see if I wanted to go shopping with her on Tuesday. As soon as I told her my answer, I could tell it was the iPod discussion happening all over again. "You saw Jordan today, and you're seeing him tomorrow too? One boyfriend dumps you, so another guy automatically moves in to take his place?"

"He's not a boyfriend. I'm just helping him run lines for *Romeo and Juliet*."

"The school isn't doing *Romeo and Juliet*."

"Yes, we are. I talked to Mrs. Shale about it and . . . well . . ."

Kate let out a huff. "She decided to do the play just because you wanted it?"

"Not just because I wanted it. I mean, Shakespeare is like eating your vegetables. It's good for you. The school needs it. In fact, you should try out for the play."

Kate ignored my suggestion. The last time I convinced her to try out with me, I got the lead in *Our Town* and she got to be one of the dead people who sit around at the cemetery waxing nostalgic about when they were alive. "So this cute new guy moves here," Kate said, "and he just coincidentally wants to be in the play with you?"

In other words, Romeo just blew down Main Street.

I couldn't tell her the truth. I couldn't tell her Jordan was plotting to get his parents back together. That would mean I'd have to tell her about Jordan's father being an actor. Besides, she'd think Jordan's attempts were foolish, and then I'd have to hear countless lectures about how I shouldn't encourage Jordan's unrealistic expectations, or how manipulating people wasn't ethical, or whatever other moral vignettes Kate could draw out of this situation. No one stands on a soapbox like Kate. It's like she has too much time on her hands, so she has become a freelance commentator on all that's wrong in the world.

The girl seriously needed a hobby.

Or at least a boyfriend to take her mind off of her lack of hobbies.

As I sat there with the phone in my hand I realized Jordan hadn't blown down Main Street for me. He'd blown down it for her. They had everything in common. Kate's dad had left her family. Jordan's dad had left his. Kate hated contact sports. Jordan ran cross-country. Kate hated guys who were insincere. Jordan said he didn't use pickup lines. Kate was a liberal. Jordan just moved from L.A. Okay, this didn't necessarily guarantee his liberalism, but for some reason that has never been clear to me but is apparent during every presidential election, people who live in big cities tend to be liberal. So probably Jordan would just nod his head and agree with her when she went off on some tangent about how capitalism was unfair to Third World countries.

It was meant to be. Or at least it would be, once I helped push things in that direction.

"Jordan is a really great guy," I told her. "I mean, how many guys would let you use their phone and then offer to drive you home after you just accused them of being a carjacker?"

"Sounds like you like him," Kate said.

"No," I answered too quickly. "I mean, I'm still not over Brendan. I can't start a new relationship yet . . . but he might be perfect for you."

"Me?"

"Sure. He's good-looking, nice, and I could tell by the way he read his Romeo lines that he's sensitive. I bet he doesn't even *watch* football on TV."

There was silence on the line. I knew Kate was weighing my words.

"I could introduce you," I said. "If you decide to try out for the play, we could all read lines together. Do you want me to ask him if it's okay for you to come over to his house to-morrow?"

Another moment of silence, and then Kate's voice came over the line sounding tentative. "He is kinda cute."

"He's way cute, Kate."

"Okay." She let out a hopeful sigh. "Ask him."

Jordan hadn't given me his phone number, but my caller ID at home still had it recorded from when he'd called me about the mall. While I got ready for work I called and casually mentioned that Kate wanted to be in the play and did he mind if she came with me to run lines?

He didn't. Then we talked about school. He asked me about people he'd met, and I gave him my unbiased opinion. Especially about Lauren Riverdale.

"Total man-stealing floozy," I said when he brought up her name. "Plus, she thinks she has fashion sense when she couldn't match a pair of shoes if they didn't come in the box together. I mean, maroon shirt and red heels? I just don't think so."

Jordan laughed at me.

"What?" I asked.

"Which condemns her more in your mind—that she stole Brendan or that she mixes up her colors?"

I hadn't mentioned Brendan's name. The phone felt suddenly heavy in my hands. "How did you know about him?"

"You're not the only one I've talked to today," he said. "That's the nice thing about small towns. Everyone knows everything about everyone else. Hey, did you really eat paste in the second grade?"

"It was Elmer's glue, and it was a dare, all right?"

He laughed again.

"What else do you know about me?"

"I heard details on several of your embarrassing moments. The soccer game in eighth grade when you accidentally took off your shorts has passed into legend status."

Okay, this is why people need to move to new towns every few years—so these types of stories don't follow them around for the rest of their lives. "Did you find out anything about my friend Kate?" I asked.

"Kate? No. I didn't ask. Why?"

"She's really nice. I think you'll like her."

There was a pause on the line. "What do you mean? Are you trying to set me up with her?"

"No. No. Heaven's no." All of those no's because he sounded like he didn't want to be set up, and there is no quicker way to get a guy to dislike a girl than to try and push him into liking her. Guys are like cats that way. They want to think they're in charge of their lives, and it's better just to humor them. "I'm only letting you know there are nice people in Three Forks—you know, as opposed to those people who ratted on me for eating glue."

Then because I knew Jordan now needed an extra incentive to look at Kate, I laid down some guy bait for him. "Besides, I wouldn't try to set up Kate. She's really particular about the guys she goes out with. It's not enough for a guy to be good-looking or popular—she's only interested if he's intelligent and loaded with class."

This is acting, not lying, so I will not be sent to hell for saying these sorts of things.

The conversation moved on, and I wasn't certain how much of the bait Jordan had taken. Tomorrow would tell.

Finally I hung up the phone and hurried to work. I came in ten minutes late. Mr. Cranston, my boss, grunted his displeasure at my arrival. I felt extra bad about this, since I'd already told him that when play rehearsals started I could only come in on Saturdays and Fridays after school. Mrs. Shale gave us Fridays off, so we had one day out of the week to accomplish anything we needed to do, like, say, homework.

Mr. Cranston had grunted a lot about my drama schedule and mumbled about how this forced other employees to work more areas in order to cover for me. Sorry, fellow Wal-Marters, blame the untidy cat toy aisle on me.

I walked to the employee break room, put my purse in my locker, and then went out onto the floor in a good mood despite Mr. Cranston's grumblings. Somehow talking to Jordan made taking a few grumbles seem worth it.

My plan for getting Jordan and Kate together on Tuesday was simple. An hour into our after-school practice, Nicki would ring my cell phone and tell me Wal-Mart had called me to work an extra shift. Someone had called in sick, and they desperately needed me to cover, yadda yadda yadda. I'd drive away and let destiny take over.

Nothing simpler, even if it did mean I had to agree to let Nicki borrow my new jean jacket and have first dibs on the shower for a week.

In drama class that day, Mrs. Shale announced that tryouts for *Romeo and Juliet* would be held on Thursday. She made it sound like she was doing us all a favor, and said that after much discussion with Principal Poure, they'd decided that despite the financial sacrifice it would cause the school, the arts were an important part of our curriculum.

Yeah. Like she hadn't already reserved a front-row seat in the auditorium for Christopher Hunter.

After drama class I wandered over to Mrs. Shale's desk while I waited for Kate and Jordan to show up. "You don't mind if I hang out for a couple of minutes, do you?" I asked her. "Jordan, Kate, and I are meeting here, then going over to Jordan's house to run lines." This was sort of name-dropping, but I figured I ought to remind Mrs. Shale I was important, just in case she had any inkling of giving Mary the role of Juliet.

"Jordan is coming here? Now?" She ran one hand across her hair and wiped away invisible specks of lint from her shirt.

"Yeah, we figure the more we go over the lines, the easier it will be to memorize them."

"Oh yes, of course." Mrs. Shale stood up and straightened papers on her desk. "That's so important when studying a role." She slid a stack of notebooks into her top desk drawer. "Especially in trying out for something as deeply layered as Shakespeare. Shakespeare is real acting. It's sophisticated. Elite." She picked up stray pencils and shoved them into an organizer on top of her desk. "You have to have talent to pull off Shakespeare." She swiped her hand across the rest of the desk, sending paper clips, staples, and scraps of paper into her top drawer, which she then shut with a muffled thud. "Will Jordan be trying out for Romeo?"

"Yeah, I guess." Although now that I thought about it, I realized he hadn't said what role he wanted. "He's worried about the language in the play. Shakespeare is hard to memorize. And then you have to figure out the right way to project a character."

"He doesn't like Shakespeare?" Mrs. Shale momentarily stopped straightening her desk and looked at me.

"Well, he didn't say he didn't *like* Shakespeare." What he'd said was more along the lines of "no one will come to watch it," but Mrs. Shale would not appreciate this prediction. "Jordan was just concerned because it would be difficult to act."

"Ohhh." Mrs. Shale drew out the word as though deeply troubled by this revelation.

"But he definitely wants to be in the play," I added. "He's really excited to try his hand at acting."

There is a fine line between diplomacy and lying, and at moments like these I like to consider myself a good diplomat.

"Well then—" Mrs. Shale started to say something else but stopped abruptly as Jordan entered the room. She stifled a little gasp, which thankfully he was too far away to hear, then stood and glided across the room. "You must be Jordan." She extended her hand to him. "I'm Chris Shale, the drama coach. I hear you'll be trying out for our play."

"Yeah. Hi. Glad to meet you." He shook her hand, then glanced at me to see what I made of the situation. I shrugged as though it were perfectly normal for a teacher to shake a student's hand that way.

"We were just discussing *Romeo and Juliet*," she said, reluctantly letting go of his hand. "Some of the students are concerned because the language is so archaic. They feel it might be hard to portray the characters well. What do you think?"

He shrugged. "It didn't make a lot of sense to me when I read it."

"Exactly," Mrs. Shale shook her head vigorously. "Well put. I'm going to look for a modernized version of the play for that very reason. We wouldn't want the audience to think it didn't make sense."

And Kate thinks I live a charmed life.

Jordan, who didn't realize the U-turn his opinion had just caused, only smiled. "Great."

"Whatever script I decide on, it will be something first-rate. All of our productions here are of the highest quality because the arts are essential to living a well-balanced life. In fact, in the banquet of life, art is the dessert, don't you think?"

Jordan nodded politely. "Sure."

Mrs. Shale smiled, letting her hand roll in front of her like she was about to warm up an orchestra. "We as actors provide the frosting on the cake."

Before Mrs. Shale could launch into further dessert metaphors, or say something that would make Jordan realize she knew who he was, I took hold of his arm and tugged him toward the door. "We really should go look for Kate now, but we'll see you later, Mrs. Shale."

Jordan followed me, and as we walked out the door Mrs. Shale called after us, "I look forward to seeing you perform on Thursday!" I knew she wasn't referring to me.

We walked a few steps down the hallway, then stopped to wait for Kate.

Jordan looked over his shoulder at the door. "She's certainly enthusiastic."

"Yeah." I didn't know what else to say. I dug through my purse until I found my car keys so my hands had something to do.

He saw my keys and shook his head. "You don't have to worry about driving. We can take my car."

"I have to drive," I said. "Otherwise you'll have to bring me back to the school parking lot to pick up my car."

"I don't mind," he said.

"That doesn't make any sense." And besides, that would interfere with my plan of pretending to go to work. I would need my car in order to leave him and Kate alone together.

Jordan lowered his voice. "You can't take your car, because I don't want my mom to see it."

"Why not?"

Jordan lowered his voice even more and leaned closer to me. "Do you remember that agreement we made where you'll let me borrow your car? This is part of the arrangement. My parents can't know you have a car exactly like mine."

I waited for him to say more, but he didn't. I waited for what he'd already said to make sense. That didn't happen either. I tilted my head at him. "What exactly are you planning to do with my car anyway?"

"You might also remember that part of the bargain is I don't tell you why I want to borrow your car."

I fingered my key chain, but didn't drop it back in my purse. "Oh, come on. You can trust me. What are you going to do?"

His gaze locked on mine, debating. I blinked my lashes back at him, trying to look innocent and trustworthy. He opened his mouth to speak, but I never got to hear his secret. Kate walked up to us, breathless, her backpack slung over her shoulders. "Hi guys. I finally made it." She smiled over at Jordan hesitantly, and I realized I hadn't introduced them.

"Jordan this is Kate. Kate this is Jordan." Destiny, this is your cue to step in and take over.

We all went in Jordan's car—which I still thought was ridiculous but which I couldn't argue about, since it involved our secret agreement and Kate was with us now. When Nicki called me in an hour, I'd just have to pretend she had called for some other reason. She'd say, "Hey, work phoned to tell you that you need to come in," and I'd say, "It's in my closet on the top shelf," and hang up. Then while we ran lines

I'd try to think of plan B in the get-Kate-and-Jordan-together strategy.

Jordan drove to a neighborhood where custom-built houses sat on one-acre lots. His was a one-story brick with ornately carved double doors and a stack of boxes sitting just inside the garage.

His mom greeted us when we came in. She wasn't what I expected. I had imagined some silicon-laden bleached blonde with diamonds dangling from her earlobes. Someone very Hollywood. Instead, she looked liked she might have been one of my mom's friends. She wore jeans and a T-shirt and not a whole lot of makeup. Still, she was pretty. Slim, brunette, and young enough to make it hard to believe she was Jordan's mom. But the look in her eye left no room for question. She gave us the mother-checking-out-her-offspring's-friends look. She seemed to approve because she smiled and told us how nice it was that we'd come over to help Jordan with his homework.

I noticed in the introductions that she went by Ms. Hunter. At another time I might not have thought anything about a woman still using her ex-husband's last name. As it was, it seemed like a sign that Jordan was right. Maybe she couldn't let go of the name, because she didn't want to let go of Jordan's dad.

We exchanged a few more pleasantries. She told us to help ourselves to chips and sodas in the kitchen, then excused herself to go to work on unpacking.

We went into the kitchen—cherrywood floor, granite countertops, and a huge bay window that overlooked a pool— and sat around the kitchen table with sodas and a bowl full of Chex Mix. Kate perched stiffly on her chair and looked at her copy of *Romeo and Juliet* instead of Jordan. You'd think someone who could argue with complete strangers during debate meets would have no trouble starting a conversation with a new kid, but she didn't even try. I decided to start on our lines and hoped she'd warm up eventually.

I mean even destiny needs something to work with.

Opening my book to Romeo and Juliet's meeting scene, I leaned toward Jordan. "You have to remember three things when reciting your lines: body language, voice inflection, and timing."

Kate ran her finger along the list of characters on the first page. "There are only four female parts in this whole play. There are seventeen male parts and only four female ones. What is Mrs. Shale thinking?"

Jordan popped some Chex into his mouth. "She's not going to find seventeen guys in your school willing to wear tights."

I set my book on the table, glancing at the dialogue while I opened a Diet Sprite. "She'll probably just have some of the girls play guy characters."

Kate fingered the pages of her book and groaned. "So not only do I have to be good enough to convince people I can act, I may have to pull off being a Franciscan friar?"

"Maybe she'll make you a nun."

"Figures," Kate flipped through the pages. "How many lines do Lady Capulet and Lady Montague have?"

Kate apparently doesn't believe in making things easy for destiny. Either that, or she has no concept as to what is involved in flirting. I would have to point out to her later that talking to, smiling over, or even looking at a guy were necessary components of the event. I turned to Jordan. "Are you ready to start?"

He took a slow sip of soda. "I thought Mrs. Shale said she

was going to get an updated version. What's the point of reading the lines if they'll all be different?"

"The wording may change but the characters will be the same, so we'll work on characterizations." I stood up with the book in one hand and motioned for him to follow me. "First off, Romeo is not sitting around a table munching snack food. Why don't you and Kate stand up and do the balcony scene."

Across the table Kate gasped. "Did you guys know this? Juliet is only thirteen!" She laid the book down on the table. "Thirteen years old, and she gets married. I mean, that is just creepy."

"Kate, do you want to read with Jordan?"

"Hold on." Kate flipped through more pages. "I'm checking to see how old Romeo is because if he's older than eighteen, it's not only creepy, it's illegal."

Jordan stood up, stretched, and opened his book. "I don't think they had the same laws in sixteenth-century Italy."

"That's not the point," Kate answered.

I really didn't want to know what her point was. I mean, my whole point at this practice was to get Kate and Jordan together, which meant it wasn't a good time for her to determine whether Romeo was taking advantage of Juliet's naïveté.

"Why don't we read through the scene first," I told Jordan, "and then you can run through it with Kate." Assuming she could do Juliet without telling Romeo off.

Jordan held the book with one hand, balancing it on his palm. "But, soft! what light through yonder window breaks?"

"You need to deliver your lines from your diaphragm," I told him.

"Diaphragm? I thought Juliet was on the balcony and Romeo was on the ground."

I took a step closer to Jordan and put my hand on his chest underneath his rib cage. "This is your diaphragm. You need to breath deep and open yourself up so everyone can hear you." I dropped my hand. "Try it again."

A phone on the table rang, but it wasn't time for Nicki's call, and I was paying such close attention to Jordan's chest—I mean, his use of his diaphragm—that I didn't think about Kate answering it until I heard her say, "Okay, I'll let Jessica know."

Then I hurried back to the table, but it was too late. By the time I got there, Kate had hung up. "Bad news. Nicki says Wal-Mart just called, and they need you to come in right away to cover a shift."

My sister apparently lives in a time warp, where twenty minutes and an hour are the same thing. I was *so* not going to let her borrow my jean jacket for doing this to me.

Jordan drove me to Wal-Mart. I told him I would call the store and tell them that I couldn't come in. I told him he could just drive me to the school, and I'd drive myself to work from there.

But no dice. He worried about me getting to Wal-Mart as soon as possible, since Kate said I was needed there "right away."

Like it was an emergency room instead of a store that sold Saran Wrap and tennis balls.

My mom says all events in life—both good and bad—are valuable for the lessons they teach you. Mom also says if you don't learn the lessons you're supposed to, life keeps giving you the same experiences over and over until you learn what you need to. I am obviously missing some big, important lesson because I'm continually finding myself in awkward situations.

Jordan left Kate at his house reading through Shakespeare—probably scouring the play for other offenses against Juliet—and dropped me off at Wal-Mart's front door. He said he'd be back in four hours so he could take me to my car at the school.

"Oh, you don't have to," I said yet again. "I can call my parents." They would wonder why in the world I was at work and my car was at the school, and probably I'd hear countless jokes about stranding myself in the Wal-Mart parking lot twice in one week, but at least I wouldn't have to hang out in the store for four hours.

"It's no problem," Jordan said. "My mom is always finding something she needs me to buy, so I'll probably have to come back tonight anyway." And then he drove off before I could argue the point further.

So I was stuck at Wal-Mart. This meant I'd have to call my parents and let them know I'd be home late so they didn't call Jordan's house wondering what was taking me so long. This meant I'd have to spend the rest of the afternoon at the place I worked without getting paid to be there, and mostly this meant I was never going to take up matchmaking as a career choice.

five

$\mathcal{J}$ didn't want to walk around the store the entire four hours. I mean, I have browsed every square inch there is to browse at Wal-Mart, and besides, I had homework to do. If I went to the break room for that long, the other employees would ask what I was doing, and then why I was here on my day off.

I was not going to tell them the truth, and I didn't have a plausible lie thought up. There was only one thing to do. I went and camped out in a stall in the women's bathroom. With my Advanced Algebra book on one knee and my notebook on the other, I did my math problems. Which would have worked out all right except it was hard to balance my calculator along with everything else on my knees, and I kept dropping it. My calculator probably picked up multiple germs and a couple of communicable diseases while down on the floor, and I wondered what the people in the stalls next to me thought of my groping around for it; but no one ever asked.

That's the nice thing about doing your homework in a bathroom stall: No one feels the need to make pointless small talk with you.

After I finished my math homework, I wrote the rough

draft of my English paper, studied my Spanish vocab words, and read the next two chapters of my history book. When all of that was finished, I still had forty-five minutes left to wait, so I got out my copy of *Romeo and Juliet* and read through it. I envisioned myself as Juliet—in love, passionate, and willing to die for the man who'd captured my heart. I saw myself on-stage in a flowing white dress, with jewels intertwined with my hair.

This is harder than one might imagine while toilets are flushing around you.

I shut my eyes and tried to block out everything else, like Mrs. Shale taught us. I tried to think like Juliet, to be her. I said her lines in my mind over and over again until I realized I was actually saying the words out loud, delivering them so they filled the bathroom.

See, there are some people who might not understand why you're doing that in a stall.

I peered out of the crack in the door to see how many people were around. Two women washed their hands at the sinks. I grimaced and scooted as far away from the door as I could, just in case either of them had X-ray vision—or at least really good vision—and could somehow tell who I was through the door crack.

Then I silently waited for them to leave the bathroom so I could sneak out undetected.

I hoped Kate appreciated all this bathroom time I'd put in for her. It's not every friend who'd hide out in a public restroom for four hours just so she could have quality flirt time with the guy she liked.

After I slunk out of the bathroom, I checked my watch. Ten minutes left until Jordan came. I decided to go wait for him outside.

When I'd taken three steps away from the bathroom, I saw Jordan walk through the front door. Two steps later, he saw me. "No blue vest today?" he asked.

"I wore a borrowed one—just put it away, in fact. I got off a few minutes early."

If God is really as strict about lying as my Sunday School teacher says he is, I'm in big trouble.

"Did you need to buy anything here?" I asked. "Or are you ready to go?"

"I'm ready," he said.

We turned to leave, but right then Mr. Cranston lumbered toward me. He held out one hand like a traffic cop, then called out, "Jessica!"

They say your life flashes before your eyes when you die. I'm not sure about that, but I do know your life—particularly the parts where you've told big, whopping lies to guys— flashes before your eyes when you're about to be exposed by your store manager.

"Mr. Cranston," I said in a half-strangled voice. Then I simultaneously tried to send him psychic messages not to say anything about my being in the store when I wasn't working and prayed for deliverance really hard.

I'm not sure of everything I promised God to get me out of this situation gracefully, but at some point in my life, I may have to become a missionary to a Third World country.

"Jessica, could you do me a favor?" Mr. Cranston asked.

"Sure," I squeaked.

"Could you check in the ladies room and tell me if any wackos are in there? I just heard from one of the customers that someone is in there talking to Romeo."

You know, I really need to be more specific when I request deliverance from God.

I felt my face reddening, but I kept my voice even. "I just came from the bathroom, and it's empty."

"Good." He shook his head. "Wackos and drug addicts. I wish they'd just stay away from the store." Then without another word he turned around and headed toward his office.

I walked to the front door without looking at Jordan, but I could hear him beside me laughing anyway. "Wackos, drug addicts, and *actors*," he said as we stepped outside. "Someone should have warned your boss about those."

I ignored him.

"Why were you practicing lines in the bathroom anyway?"

"Because the hygiene aisle was already taken."

He laughed again as we walked across the parking lot. "Man, talk about method acting. You're either really dedicated or you should be committed someplace. I'm not sure which."

I shook my head. "Just add this day to the list of my embarrassing moments."

He opened his car door for me, which would have been very gentlemanly if he hadn't added, "This one is my car," as he did it.

I mean, really.

With my arms folded, I waited for him to walk around to his side of the car. When he slid in and started the engine, I said, "You never did tell me *your* most embarrassing moment."

"And I never will, either."

"Oh, come on."

He shook his head, the humor draining from his expression. I could tell he was thinking about that moment. And it wasn't good.

I decided to change the subject. "Did you and Kate rehearse much?"

"Naw, but we did agree we both hated Shakespeare, although for different reasons. She thinks he's a sexist, opinionated misogynist, and I think the way he kept rhyming things is really annoying."

I'd just spent four hours in a bathroom, and Kate had spent the time talking about Shakespeare's view on women? The girl was hopeless.

"I'm definitely not ready for tryouts," he said. "I can read the words, but I don't know how to act them. I mean what do I do with my body while I'm saying stuff? I tried to wave my hand around a little while I spoke; but it didn't feel natural, and it probably looked stupid."

"Your body language problem," I said.

"Yeah, whatever. Can we get together and go over this some more? You didn't really have a chance to help me with it today."

The only time left was tomorrow, and that's when I was laying my trap for Brendan. But how could I say no to Jordan after I hadn't helped him today? He needed my expertise. The poor boy was resorting to hand-waving in an attempt to perform his lines. "I guess we could go over it right after school," I said. Because Brendan had football practice after school so wouldn't come over till later. "But it has to be at my house because I have to make cookies for . . . something."

"Your house it is then," Jordan said, and he smiled.

Every time I saw Kate the next day, she talked about Jordan. By lunchtime I'd heard it all. Twice. Jordan was so nice. Jordan was so handsome. Jordan had offered to put a Pima curse on Shakespeare for her.

I unwrapped my sandwich. "Indians have curses for dead people?"

She made one of those coughing noises that isn't really a cough but a way to tell you that you just said something stupid. "Of course not, Jessica, don't be so culturally insensitive. He was joking. He has a wonderful sense of humor."

Yeah. Right. He was perfect, and I was getting sick of hearing about it. I ate my sandwich in silence while she tried to repeat, verbatim, their entire conversation from yesterday.

"I think he likes me," she finished off with a sigh. "You can always tell by how much attention a guy pays to you. When I was with him, he made me feel—you know—important. Like what I thought mattered."

Maybe Jordan is just the type of person who makes people feel important, I nearly said. After all, he always made me feel like I mattered too. He took my advice about clothes, shared a secret with me, and laughed at my jokes.

The sandwich felt like dust in my mouth. Jordan made me feel special, and I'd handed him over to Kate.

Because I was in love with Brendan, I reminded myself. So I shouldn't be thinking of Jordan that way, especially since I'd just handed him over to Kate. I should encourage her guy-getting attempts. I should tell her, for example, that Jordan was coming over to my house after school, and invite her along— even if that meant I then had to watch her making jokes about Shakespeare with Jordan, like it was some exclusive club just the two of them belonged to.

I took a sip of milk, fingered the straw, and then made myself speak. "Jordan said he wanted to run lines again after school. We're going to my house. Do you want to come?"

"Want to? Definitely. But the Spanish Club is electing officers today, and Senor Gomez wants me to be secretary. Besides, in English class Mrs. Shale said she'll get a totally modern version of *Romeo and Juliet*. It will all be different. But she said she'd give us a few minutes before tryouts to read over the stuff to familiarize ourselves with it. So, you know, Jordan shouldn't worry about it." She leaned forward, tapping her fingers on the table excitedly. "All day I've tried to think of an excuse to go up and talk to him, and that's it. I'll tell him what Mrs. Shale told us, so he won't have to worry about running lines with you after all."

She said this as though it would be a great relief to Jordan, as though I'm to be avoided whenever possible.

I tried not to squeeze my milk carton, but somehow milk managed to shoot up my straw and spill on the table anyway. I didn't say anything else to Kate. I didn't have to. She was back to talking about how wonderful Jordan was.

*A*s the day wore on, it ticked me off more and more that Kate wanted to cancel my acting session with Jordan. I mean, she had no right to do that. Just because she couldn't come didn't mean he didn't need the help. The boy didn't even have pickup lines. What did he know about being a Romeo?

My mind circled around this issue instead of fluttering around the idea of Brendan coming to see me. And Brendan was coming to see me. I'd sent him my E-mail this morning, since I knew it would be hard to send it after school while Jordan was over. Brendan must have already read it because when I walked by him on my way to Advanced Algebra, his gaze followed every step I took. He stood beside Lauren, hanging around the drinking fountain like it was some sort of social event, but he watched me. His lips started to form words; they nearly hung in the air, then he glanced at Lauren and didn't say them.

There is only one reason you don't say, "Hey, thanks for telling me about my history book. I'll be by to pick it up later," and that is because you don't want your girlfriend to know you're coming over to my house.

So he was coming.

Whether Jordan was coming or not, I wasn't sure, and my thoughts went something like: *I'll wear the gold earrings Brendan got me last Christmas and have his favorite CD playing in the background, and . . . Does Jordan like country music? Do American Indians in general hate country music because the stars sometimes wear cowboy hats and boots?* I mean, maybe the whole cowboy thing stirred up bad memories for them. But then again, maybe it was stupid of me to even wonder about that. Music preferences were an individual thing, right?

And would Jordan be offended if I noted the cultural difference between us, or would he be offended if I didn't? Kate, who was the queen of all that was politically correct, probably knew the answer to this question, but I wasn't about to ask her. She was the one who was trying to uninvite him from my house.

I was actually surprised and immensely relieved when Jordan showed up at my locker after school. Kate apparently hadn't found the opportunity to talk to him after all.

We drove to my house in separate cars—although if Brendan hadn't been coming over, I would have insisted on taking Jordan in my car just to be difficult. As it was, I had to run lines with Jordan, get the cookies going, and change into a stunning outfit, all before Brendan arrived.

The first thing I did when we got to my house was banish Nicki to her room. She claimed she wanted to watch us act; but I knew she would just hang around giggling, so I threatened not to let her have any cookies unless she left us alone.

Then Jordan and I made up a double batch of chocolate chip—a double batch because it only seemed fair to send Jordan home with some, since he was helping to make them.

As we measured, stirred, and talked about school I wondered what he would think if he knew he was helping me make cookies as a way to recapture my old boyfriend. I also wondered what Jordan would look like riding a horse against the setting sun, deerskin trousers on his legs and war paint smeared across his chest. Usually I didn't think those thoughts consecutively, but sometimes I did, and after a while the image of Jordan on a horse sort of overtook thoughts of Brendan altogether.

I tried to banish this line of thinking by telling myself American Indians had probably never dressed like that. Hollywood most likely just put them in movies that way because they knew women audience members loved to see shirtless guys running around on horses.

Jordan, for example, would look stunning on a palomino.

After we put the cookies in the oven, we went into the family room to work on the play. Dad was at work, Mom was out running errands, and Nicki had taken the phone to her room and thus might never reemerge. The house seemed strangely silent, and I suddenly felt awkward standing alone with Jordan.

"So you need help with your motions?" I asked him.

"Yeah. What am I supposed to do with my body while I deliver my lines?"

"Your body . . ." I let my gaze momentarily wander, then snapped it back to his face. "It depends on your emotion. How do you want to feel? I mean, how do you want your character to feel?" I glanced over at the kitchen. "Is it hot in here? Do you think the oven heated up the room too much?"

"I'm fine."

Yes, he was, and I had to stop noticing that aspect of him. Jordan needed help with his acting. That's all.

I took a step back from him. "So what emotion are you trying to convey to the audience?"

He shrugged. "I'm attracted to Juliet."

"Right. So how do you act when you're attracted to some-one?"

More shrugging, this time with a look of exasperation thrown in.

"You're making this harder than it is. Here, let's pretend you and I have just met at a party, and you want to get my phone number. Don't worry about what you're going to say. What you say isn't important. Your body language is what we're working on. So go ahead and talk to me."

He nodded, put his hands on his hips, then seemed un-happy with that and folded his arms instead. "Hey."

"Hey," I said back to him.

He took a step closer to me. "Great band, huh?"

"Yeah, they're really good. Um, what kind of band are they? I mean, do you hate country music?"

"What?" he asked, then put his hands back on his hips. "Is that what you'd really say to me at a party?"

"No, but I just wondered what kind of music you like."

"Me as Jordan, or me as Romeo?"

"You. Jordan."

"Oh. Country is okay. I like rock too. I'm partial to oldies." He dropped his hand from his hips. "Can I get back to being Romeo now?"

"Sure." I smiled at him. I liked oldies too.

He took another step closer to me. He wore the blue shirt I'd picked out for him. The color looked rich and vibrant against his skin. I suppressed the urge to reach over and smooth out its wrinkles.

He gazed around the room as though checking out the invisible party. "So, do you like to dance?"

"Yes. Have you ever ridden a horse?"

He cocked his head at me. "What kind of answer is that? Are you purposely trying to throw me off?"

"No. I just think you'd look great on a horse."

He took a final step toward me. We were now so close if I reached out my hands just a little, I could touch him. With my gaze I traced the line his cheekbones made against his face.

His voice was low. "That isn't what you'd say to a guy you'd just met."

"I might," I said. "If the guy was hot."

He took hold of my hand, interlacing his fingers with mine. "What else would you say?"

"You're the one who's supposed to say things. You're Romeo."

"Right." He pulled me closer to him, almost into an embrace, then whispered into my ear, "As soon as I met you, I could tell there was something special about you. I'm glad we're together right now." He bent down and kissed me, and I kissed him back.

Because I was Juliet.

Because I was helping Jordan with acting, which he'd apparently mastered really fast.

Because I wanted to.

Finally I pulled away from him, breathed deeply, and ran a hand through my hair. "See, once you get into character, you don't really have to worry about body language. It's, you know, finding the right motivation that's the key."

He cocked his head and smiled at me. "Jessica, I wasn't acting." Then the smile dropped from his lips. "Were you?"

"No, but—" At that moment I saw Kate's face, not Brendan's: Kate, who had spent the entire day telling me how wonderful Jordan was. Kate, who'd been trying to find a way to go up and talk to him. Kate, who trusted me.

"I do like you," I said softly, "but Kate likes you too. I actually encouraged her to like you. I can't just take you away now."

His eyebrows raised. He looked at me, then beyond me as though searching for answers somewhere in the room. "If you like me, why would you encourage your best friend to like me?"

"Because . . ." I was stupid, blind, and had convinced myself I wanted revenge on Lauren and affirmation from Brendan. Because I was trying to do something nice for my best friend.

I plopped down on the couch. "I thought Kate was more your type. I want to be an actress, and you don't like the profession. She's a liberal, and you're from California. Besides, Kate thinks everything good always happens to me. It just seemed to be her turn to have the new guy like her."

He tilted his head at me like he couldn't quite follow my logic. "I didn't know girls took turns having guys like them. And what does living in California have to do with which political party you belong to?"

"You're not a liberal?"

"No."

I threw my hands up in the air. "Well, you should have told me that before I gave you to Kate."

"You gave me to Kate?" he repeated.

"Yes, that's what I've been trying to tell you."

The doorbell rang. I waited for someone else to get it, then remembered I was the only one of the family around. I stood up, annoyed at the interruption, and strode out of the room. "This will just take a second," I told Jordan's back because he was still staring at the couch in disbelief.

I walked from the family room, through the living room, and flung open the door. Brendan stood on the porch step with a half smile plastered on his face. "Hi, Jessica."

I blinked at him for a moment, not realizing why he stood at my door. Then I remembered. "Oh, your book," I said. I hadn't expected him until much later. "Why aren't you at football practice?"

"I got off early and knew you wanted me to come over and talk."

I clutched the doorknob and stared at him. "Oh?"

He nodded, as though pleased at himself for figuring me out. "Otherwise you would have just brought the book to school and put it in my locker. After all, you know my combination."

"Oh," I said for the third time because apparently it is the only word I can retrieve from my vocabulary when I'm flustered. "I don't. I mean, I know your locker combination, but I don't have to talk to you about anything." The words didn't make much sense, but I didn't clarify myself. I just wanted to return to Jordan. "I'll go get your book."

Even though I hadn't invited him in, Brendan walked through the door. "Are those chocolate chip cookies I smell?" He gave me a knowing smile.

I'm over you, I wanted to tell him. As of this moment I don't care if you and Lauren elope. Jordan was standing in the family room processing every stupid thing I'd said to him. I needed to get back to him so we could finish our conversation. "Your book is in my room. I'll go get it."

Taking the stairs two at a time, I ran to my room, grabbed the book from my dresser, and dashed back downstairs. I put it in Brendan's hands, breathlessly. "There you go. Well, see you around."

He tucked the book under his arm and tilted his head at me, questioningly. "That's all you wanted to say to me?"

"Pretty much, yeah. Good-bye."

He let out an exasperated sigh. "Jessica, you don't have to be this way."

"What way?"

"You can tell me whatever it is you wanted to say to me."

I held out my hands in front of me and shook my head. "I don't have anything to say."

Then Brendan looked beyond me, and his eyes narrowed. I turned and saw that Jordan had walked out of the family room and into the living room. He stood a few feet back, arms folded, watching the two of us.

The muscles on the side of Brendan's mouth twitched, but he managed to pull off a stiff smile. "Is this your new boyfriend?"

Jordan walked the rest of the distance to us. "No, I'm not Jessica's boyfriend. I'm the guy she likes but is giving to Kate because it's her best friend's turn to have a boyfriend."

"Jordan . . ." I said.

"What?" Brendan asked.

Jordan held up his hand, a gesture of disbelief. "You didn't know girls could give guys away either? Apparently they have an entire system set up that we don't know about. Just think of all the effort we could have saved ourselves if we had known."

I put a hand on my hip. "There is no need to be sarcastic about this." Then to Brendan I said, "This is really not a good time for me to talk with you, but . . . um . . . you have your book and good luck on your history test." Then I smiled my please-leave-now smile, and he finally got the message.

"Great. Good-bye," he said tightly. Then he turned around, strode out the door, and slammed it shut. Which I thought was entirely uncalled for. I mean, what did he have to be mad about?

Jordan walked back into the family room and picked up his backpack. "Maybe I should leave too."

I followed him, then stood in front of him blocking his way. A knot the size of a soccer ball formed in my stomach. I'd done everything wrong. I hadn't explained things the way I should have. "No, Jordan, don't go."

He didn't try to push his way around me, just stood there staring into my eyes like he could squeeze the truth out of them. "Why should I stay, Jessica?"

I looked at my shoes. I looked at his shoes. I took a step toward him. He didn't move. The question hung in the air like mist on a rainy day.

"I'll explain it to Kate," I said, then took both of his hands in mine. "Maybe I want to keep you after all."

He smiled, and with that one gesture the tenseness be-tween us evaporated. He pulled me into a hug. It felt so right to lean up against him, to hear his heart beat through the shirt I'd picked out for him.

Jordan and I didn't work on drama much that night, but we did go out to dinner and a movie. Afterward Jordan told me personal tidbits about the actors in the film, like who gave out full-size candy bars at Halloween and who stiffed little kids with miniature Tootsie Rolls.

I let Jordan kiss me good night on the doorstep despite my

personal rule of never kissing a guy on the first date. I mean, since we'd already kissed in my family room, it somehow didn't seem like that rule should apply. Besides, how can you not kiss a guy good night when he's perfect for you? And Jordan was perfect for me.

I'd just have to explain it to Kate.

six

J'd never dreaded seeing Kate before. The next day at school, every time I thought about her, my stomach did this weird clenching thing, like a spring had broken in the vicinity of my belly button. I knew I'd have to tread softly to spare her feelings. I'd have to point out she'd only liked Jordan because I'd hyped him up. She didn't really know him. She'd find someone else. These things happened.

Still, I couldn't look at her when she walked up to the lunch table.

"Guess what Mrs. Shale told us about the play?" She set her tray down with a hurried clank. Two tomatoes rolled off the top of her salad.

"What?"

"We're not doing *Romeo and Juliet* after all. We're doing *West Side Story.*"

For the first time since school started my mind momentarily left What-do-I-tell-Kate-about-Jordan mode and concentrated on acting. "*West Side Story?* Isn't that a musical?"

"Yep."

"So are we going to have to sing at tryouts?" I can sing, but reading music is a mysterious art form, like calligraphy, and unicycling, which I'm incapable of. I need to hear a song, several times, before I can even attempt to sing it. Then I need to sing it several more times until I've memorized all the hard parts and know how to get around them. If I don't have enough breath left during the high parts—well, let's just say my sister uncharitably nicknamed me the shrieking Madonna after a particularly disastrous Christmas pageant five years ago. Or as a couple of the shepherds put it: " 'Silent Night' could have used a little more silence."

Kate shrugged her shoulders. "Mrs. Shale didn't say anything about singing, but that doesn't mean she won't make us."

"She should have given us a little bit of warning." I took out my sandwich and laid it on top of its plastic bag. "I bet Mary knows how to read music."

"Mary hardly knows how to read English. Mrs. Shale only gives her parts because of her father's job."

"And her looks," I said. Mary had a damsel-in-distress beauty that guys loved, not to mention a bra size whose letter is considerably closer to Z than mine.

"You're pretty too, so you have nothing to worry about," Kate said. "Besides, it's just a play."

People who say, "It's just a play," don't understand. There's no point in trying to explain it to them. So instead, Kate and I pooled all of our knowledge about *West Side Story*. It was loosely based on the idea of *Romeo and Juliet*, but set in some inner city in the fifties. Instead of feuding families, rival gangs called the Sharks and the Jets fought over street turf. A girl named Maria from one group fell in love with a guy named Tony from the other, and like Romeo and Juliet, they wanted to stay out of the fighting but got dragged into it by everyone else. Tony went to stop a rumble and ended up accidentally killing Maria's brother, Bernardo. In the end, one of Bernardo's friends shot Tony.

All that, with peppy little song and dance numbers added.

"Do you think she'll make us dance at tryouts?" I asked.

"I don't know why you're so worried." Kate nibbled on a piece of broccoli from her salad. "Mrs. Shale knows you can sing and dance, but she's only seen me be a dead person in *Our Town*. Jordan and I are going to be the ones at a disadvantage."

Jordan. His name immediately brought me back to the problem at hand.

I looked at my watch. We only had ten more minutes until our next classes. It wasn't enough time. I'd put it off till later. I'd tell her while we were waiting for tryouts.

Only that was mean. You didn't want to be thinking about news like that when you had to concentrate on song and dance numbers. I had to tell her now.

I took a breath. I cleared my throat and fiddled with my lunch sack. "About Jordan . . ." I started. "You see, I talked to him after school yesterday . . ."

Kate studied my face for a moment, then let out a sigh. "He likes someone else, doesn't he?"

"Well, yes."

"Figures." She dropped her fork onto her plate. "He was too cute to stay single for long. Which of the Three Forks flirts got her talons into him?"

More fiddling with my lunch sack. How should I put this?

Kate's gaze grew hard as she looked at me. My expressive face was getting me in trouble again. "Is it you?" she demanded.

"I didn't try to like him," I said. "I was all set to try and win Brendan back, but then I realized you were right about

Brendan. He *is* arrogant and untrustworthy. See, I'm doing what you've always told me to do. I'm raising my standards where guys are concerned."

She didn't crack a smile at my joke, but I hadn't expected her to. I just hurried on with my explanation. "I know you liked him too, but you never really got to know him. He's much more my type than yours. It turns out he's not a liberal, or a vegetarian." I knew this last bit because he'd ordered chicken Parmesan at Applebee's. "And he thinks guys should always pay for dates." I knew this because I'd offered to pay for the movie, since he'd paid for dinner. "You think everything should be equal between the sexes, so that would be one more thing you'd have to argue about."

Kate tapped her hands against the table. Her lips drew into a tight line. "Don't pretend you did this for me," she said. "You saw what you wanted and took it, just like you take everything. You've never had to do without anything your whole life, have you, Jessica?"

She didn't wait for me to answer. She picked up her lunch tray and walked off. I watched her go, my cheeks stinging as though they'd been slapped. I had anticipated disappointment, but I'd never expected this much anger. *It isn't fair to act this way,* I wanted to yell after her, *when you only liked him for two days.*

Instead, I said nothing at all. It took all of my effort to talk myself out of crying. I couldn't cry now. I only had five minutes to get to my next class.

Jordan met me at the drama room after school, and we walked together to the auditorium for tryouts. This was particularly nice, since I'd avoided talking to everybody else since lunch. Despite my acting ambitions, I knew I couldn't pull off acting like me—the normal me that is. The me that was happy. I kept on thinking of the things I wanted to say to Kate—like: *This isn't about Jordan, is it? This is about jealousy. What do you want me to do, fail at things to make you feel better?*

Despite her barbs now and again about my charmed life, I'd always thought she was happy for my successes. How long had her resentment been at the breaking point?

I half expected she wouldn't come to audition at all, but when Jordan and I walked in, she was already sitting in one of the plastic audience chairs—along with about one hundred other kids, most of them girls. Some talked with their friends, but a couple dozen read over sheets of stapled paper.

We hardly ever have this many people come to watch the productions, let alone try out for them.

I walked to the stage with Jordan, wondering what other club was meeting here now and why Mrs. Shale hadn't told them to leave. When we reached the stage, I looked for a stack of paper with the tryout lines, but the only thing sitting on the stage was Mrs. Shale's purse and jacket. She stood by the piano talking with Mrs. Cluff, the music teacher, then saw us and strode over. A big smile spread across her face— a smile directed toward Jordan, since she never even glanced at me.

"How nice to see you here," she said. "We'll start in a minute."

"Where are the papers with the tryout lines?" I asked.

"I ran out." Her gaze swept over the audience. "It's a wonderful turnout, isn't it? We've never had this much interest before. Mary is in the copy room right now, running off some more sheets." She sighed happily, and then turned her gaze back to Jordan. "As usual, we have more girls than guys here. I hope you don't mind doing multiple readings."

He shrugged. "Whatever you need me to do."

Her smile took on a hungry look. She took a step closer to him. "I can see you as Tony . . . or maybe Bernardo . . . Do you sing?"

"Not much."

"The music teacher can work with you." Another smile. His mother probably didn't smile at him this much. "Well, I'd better get things started."

Jordan and I found two seats in the back. I looked at all the heads in front of me. Tryouts were going to take forever. Why in the world had all these girls shown up, and more importantly, could any of them act?

I had considered Mary my only real competition, but now . . .

Three rows ahead of me, Lauren and her cheerleading squad sat giggling about something. Didn't they have practice after school? What were they doing here?

Mrs. Shale called a couple of people who already had papers to come up and perform part of a scene. I watched for a little bit of each read, just long enough to reassure myself I could still do a better job. Then I talked with Jordan. He told me more people had come up today to introduce themselves to him than in all of his previous life put together.

"That's because small-town folk are friendly," I told him.

"Or just really bored," he said.

Mary came back to the auditorium carrying papers. She handed out stacks to each person who sat at the end of the row so that person could pass them down the aisle. Except for our aisle. She scooted past three people just to give Jordan one.

"Here's a script," she said.

He took it and laid it on his lap. "Thanks."

"Good luck on your reading." She tilted her head so her

brown hair brushed against her shoulders. Her lips fell half open into a seductive pout. I wanted to smack her. Instead, I held out my hand. "Hey, Mary, can I get a script too?"

She pulled one off the top of the stack and shoved it at me, then turned back to Jordan. "The scene with Maria and Tony is on the front page. Bernardo's scene is toward the back."

"Thanks," he said again.

"I'm Mary East, by the way."

He nodded. "Right. You introduced yourself to me this morning."

"Right." She laughed as though she'd said something funny, and I wondered exactly how she'd introduced herself to him. "It will be great to have you in the cast."

"Thanks." A moment of silence ensued. A normal person would have returned to passing out scripts. Mary stood in front of Jordan like he was a painting she'd stopped by to admire.

"I'm trying out for the part of Maria," she said.

"Good luck," he told her.

She giggled again and finally left.

Jordan leaned closer to me. "See, I'm not sure that much friendliness is normal."

"Mary isn't friendly. She's hitting on you because you're cute and new here. Therefore you haven't learned yet that she's vain, manipulative, and has several dead bodies buried in her backyard."

"She has what in the backyard?"

"Well, that may just be speculation on my part, but I've been suspicious of her since the third grade when she stole my library book. You can't trust someone who nabs your copy of *Misty of Chincoteague*, and so you have to pay for it."

"I see." Jordan flipped through his pages, skimming the lines.

I tried to familiarize myself with Maria's lines, and not think about Mary at all. In my mind I saw Maria at the dance. Young, hopeful, and with long blond hair like mine. Dang. Maria was Puerto Rican and definitely brunette. Would Mrs. Shale penalize me for having blond hair? I could always wear a wig or dye it. I'd tell her this when I went up.

Jordan flipped from one page to the next. "And to think I complained about Shakespearean English."

"What?"

"Listen to how these gang members speak: 'Great, Daddy-o!'" He turned to another page. "'Riga tiga tum tum.'" Two pages later. "'Cracko, jacko!' What does that even mean—*cracko, jacko*?"

I shrugged. "Sounds like the punch line to a bad Michael Jackson joke."

"We're going to look stupid saying this stuff."

"Not me. Maria doesn't have a foul mouth like you bad-boy gang members."

Over the top of his script, Jordan glared at me.

I nudged his knee with mine. "Don't worry. Once you get up onstage and the audience is out there cheering for you, you'll see why I love drama."

Jordan flipped to another page. "Hey, we gang members get cool names too—Action, A-rab, Chino, Pepe—who wouldn't be afraid of a Pepe?"

"I think that's pronounced 'Pep-ay,'" I said, "and not 'Peep,' or, you know, anything else."

He didn't answer me, but instead went back to his script, mouthing the lines silently.

After a few minutes Mrs. Shale called Jordan up. He took the stage casually, as though not even nervous. I, along with every other girl in the auditorium, watched him breathlessly.

He read the scene with Lauren, and then again with four other girls. He wasn't bad the first time, but by the fifth time he was good. His voice became louder, and he spoke with the right amount of emotion. He even put some body movement into it. He probably would have gotten a part even if Mrs. Shale hadn't been predisposed to adore him.

The other surprise was that Lauren could act. As she looked up at Jordan and read her lines, you could almost see the stars forming in her eyes. I hadn't expected anything so remarkable from someone whose main talent thus far had consisted of leg kicks and synchronized clapping.

To make matters worse, Lauren had brown hair. It would be bad enough to lose the part of Maria to Mary. It would kill me to lose the part to Lauren.

After Jordan finished reading with three more girls, Mrs. Shale let him go. He walked back to our seats and plopped down next to me with a smile. "How did I do?"

"Good enough that I predict you'll be saying 'Daddy-o' and 'cracko, jacko' sometime in the near future."

He could have left then. Who knew how long it would take until I had a turn to read. But he didn't. He sat next to me.

Lauren left her group of friends and walked down the aisle. I assumed she was going home, since she'd already read; but she walked over to us and sat in the chair next to Jordan. She smiled at him till he looked over at her.

"Jordan, you did really well as Tony."

He nodded at her. "Thanks, I've always wanted to belong to a singing, dancing street gang."

She laughed a light, tinkly laugh. I hated her all over again.

"Oh, I haven't introduced myself. I'm Lauren."

And apparently I was invisible because no one seemed to notice me sitting by Jordan.

Lauren ran her acrylic nails through her hair. "Everyone thinks you'll get the part of Tony."

"Well, Mrs. Shale hasn't heard me sing yet."

"I'm sure you sing beautifully," Lauren said.

I wanted to yell, "You already got your quota of my boyfriends. Go away!" Instead, I just glared at her, which she didn't see because her eyes were magnetized to Jordan's face.

She leaned toward him. "I bet you've learned a lot of great acting techniques from your father, haven't you?"

Jordan's head jerked back with surprise. "What?"

"Your father," Lauren cooed. "Isn't your father Christopher Hunter?"

He paused as though he didn't want to answer. "Who told you that?"

She shrugged. "Everyone knows. Even the teachers were talking about it. They say he's going to come up and see the play."

The teachers. Mrs. Shale. Mrs. Shale had told everyone about Jordan's father. A wave of nausea swept over me. Even my toenails felt sick.

Unfortunately, I hadn't been rendered invisible, because Jordan reached over and took hold of my hand. Still without looking at me, he said, "Will you excuse us for a minute? I need to talk to Jessica privately." Then he stood up and half pulled me out of the auditorium.

Once we got outside, he did look at me, and then I wished he hadn't. The anger glimmered in his eyes. His jaw was clamped tight. He shook his head. "I can't believe you told people about my father. I trusted you. I specifically asked you not to tell anyone."

"I only told Mrs. Shale," I said weakly. "And I only did that because she was going to cancel the play altogether. I couldn't let her do that. You wanted your father to come and see you perform."

"I also wanted to be a normal teenager, Jessica. I didn't want to spend my senior year being some peculiarity."

"You're not a peculiarity. People like you. Is that such a bad thing?"

More head shaking. "People don't like me. They like my father. And now I'll never know whether they would have liked me."

I felt pinned to the wall by his gaze. The way he looked at me hurt.

"I'm so sorry," I gulped. "I asked Mrs. Shale not to tell anyone. I thought I could trust her."

"Well, I guess we know the truth about both of you now."

Another pin. This time through my heart.

He took a step closer to me and lowered his voice. "Tell me the truth about one thing, Jessica. Just promise you'll be honest in what you say next."

I nodded numbly.

"Did you want the play to go on so I could be in it or so you could be in it?"

My cheeks burned. It was hard to breathe. I couldn't answer.

His eyes narrowed, and he shook his head again. "I thought so." He gave me one last disappointed look, then turned and walked out of the school.

$\mathcal{J}$'m not sure how long I stood there, watching him leave and then watching nothing at all. It's hard to realize you just messed up your life. It's even harder to realize you messed up someone else's. I wanted desperately to set things right, but how could I? People knew about his father. I couldn't undo that. I couldn't think of anything that would make this even a little bit better. Finally, I walked back into the auditorium.

When I did, Kate took the stage. She read Anita's part, the woman who was Maria's best friend and Bernardo's girlfriend. While she spat out venomous lines against the gang that killed her boyfriend she glared at me. Her chest heaved in angry rhythm to her words, and the emotion poured from her lips.

Take a number, Kate, today everyone hates me.

After Kate read, Mrs. Shale called me up for my turn. Walking to the stage, I tried to keep my hands steady so the paper wouldn't shake between my fingers. It was her fault. The reason everyone knew Jordan's secret, the reason approximately half the girls in the school had shown up for tryouts, the reason the guy I liked had just walked away from me—it was Mrs. Shale's fault. How could she have done this to Jordan? To me?

Mrs. Shale sat in the front row. Her notebook lay in her lap. She gripped her pen like it was an orchestra wand. "You may begin when you're ready," she told me.

I wasn't ready. I couldn't be a young girl in love at a dance. Nothing drama class had ever taught me could help me shelve my rage. It brimmed inside of me, seeping out into the air I breathed.

I read the first line, and thought: *You betrayed me, Mrs. Shale.* I read the second. *How could you do this to me?* I read the third. *You're an adult. You're a teacher. You're not supposed to tell students' secrets.*

My performance stank. I read the part as though Maria had violent tendencies and Tony and several other members of the cast would be strangled and strewn across the dance floor before the night ended.

As I finished reading my last line the guy playing Tony took a step back from me. I had gripped the script so hard that it lay crinkled in my hands.

Mrs. Shale stared at me, tapping the top of her pen against her teeth. "Well . . . that was an interesting interpretation of Maria. Who wants to read next?"

I stepped over to the edge of the stage. "Can I talk to you privately for a minute?"

Perhaps because I was one of her drama students, or perhaps because she was tired of sitting for so long and wanted to stretch her legs, she agreed. We stepped into a small room offstage where props were stored.

I had never yelled at an adult before, let alone someone who would not only determine my grade in drama but also which, if any, part I got in the school play. Emotion whirled in my throat.

"What is it, Jessica?" Her words were impatient, not sympathetic.

My hands shook, so I crossed my arms across my chest and tucked them close to my body. "I asked you not to tell anyone about Jordan's father. I told you he didn't want anyone to know, but you told, didn't you? Everyone knows. That's why all these girls came here today. They think if they're in the play, they'll get to meet Christopher Hunter."

She made a little tsking sound, as though I was being unreasonable. "I told you I had to ask the principal for more funding. Naturally, I had to tell him about Jordan's father. He's the reason Mr. Poure even agreed to let us put on the play. One donation from Christopher Hunter could keep our arts program alive for years." She gave my hand a pat like a mother reassuring a child. "Jordan has no reason to hide his father or be embarrassed about anything. He should be proud. Besides, everyone was going to find out when his father came to see the show anyway. We just let everyone know a bit early."

"No," I said. "*We* didn't let everyone know. *You* did. You told, after I asked you not to. It doesn't matter what you thought or why you did it. You didn't have the right to make that decision for Jordan." My voice rose of its own accord. I was halfway to hysteria, mostly because I knew everything I said applied to me too. "It was his secret, not yours."

Mrs. Shale pulled herself up straighter. "I only told the principal. And his secretary. And of course, Mrs. Cluff because she's the music teacher. I only told the people I had to. If Jordan is upset, I'll talk to him tomorrow. But as for you—" She held up one finger to silence me. "You answer to me, and not the other way around. You'd do well to remember that if you want a part in our cast." She pulled the pen from behind her ear, clutched her notebook in the other hand as though it were a flyswatter, and stormed out of the room.

She probably went back to sit in front of the stage, but I'm not sure. I didn't check before I ran out of the school.

seven

My mother has often tried to comfort me with the phrase "Things always look better in the morning." The next morning was not one of those times. I had called Jordan twice after tryouts to tell him I was sorry. To tell him I'd been a jerk. To see if there was some Herculean feat I could do to earn his forgiveness. He never answered. Finally I left him a message trying to detail all of the above. I asked him if we could still be friends. I asked him to please, please call me.

He never called. I took my phone with me to school, even though it's against the rules, just in case he text messaged me.

When I got to my locker, I saw Kate sitting on the floor doing algebra homework. She looked up with surprise while I twirled my combination. "You look awful."

"Thanks."

She let out a sigh. "I didn't mean it that way. I just meant . . . well, you know what I meant."

"I suppose you meant I look awful. Was there some hidden message that I missed?"

Kate snapped her book shut, picked it up, then stood and leaned on the locker beside mine. "I meant I can tell you feel rotten about our fight. So do I. Let me apologize first and tell you I shouldn't have yelled at you about Jordan. It's not worth it to let a guy ruin our friendship." She held one hand out, as though giving me something. "Besides, after tryouts I heard all about his Hollywood connection, so I can see why you said he was more your type than mine. I mean, you want to be an actress, and I want to be a Supreme Court justice. What I'm trying to say is if you go out with Jordan, it's okay with me."

"Thanks." I shoved my backpack into my locker and got out my notebook for first period. "But you don't have to worry about Jordan. He broke up with me yesterday."

"Yesterday?"

"Yeah. I wasn't supposed to tell anyone about Jordan's father, but I told Mrs. Shale. She told an undisclosed number of people. I'm not exactly sure how many, but it's somewhere between three and the entire school population. So, you know, it's my fault everyone knows, and he's not speaking to me anymore."

Her mouth formed a sad little "Oh," and then suddenly her eyebrows shot up. "Wait a minute, is that why you look depressed this morning? It's because Jordan fought with you, not because I fought with you?"

I tapped my fingers against my locker door. "It's not a contest, Kate. I didn't consult the dark circles under my eyes to see whether they're there for you or for Jordan. I just wish yesterday never happened."

My voice cracked, and Kate put her sympathetic face back on. "Right. Me too. Let's just say yesterday never happened between us, and those dark circles will vanish. The bags under your eyes might take longer."

"Thanks," I said again.

"I know what will cheer you up. Let's go see if Mrs. Shale posted who got the parts for the play."

I was not entirely certain this would cheer me up. I shut my locker slowly, and we drifted down the hallway toward the drama room. I held my books tightly against my chest. "I yelled at Mrs. Shale at tryouts, did a horrible job, and she told me off. Well, not in that order, but she's probably the one who caused the bags under my eyes. So what kind of part do you think I'll get?"

Kate laughed as we walked. "A big one because you're still a good actress, and Mrs. Shale knows it. You have nothing to worry about. I'm the one whose only experience in drama is playing a dead person."

"It's not the size of the part that matters," I told Kate. Because I'd said it to her so many times during the production of *Our Town,* it had become our own mantra. "It's how well you do your part."

$\mathcal{A}$s it turns out, I lied to Kate during *Our Town.* There are many, many things that matter about a part, especially its size. Also, the phrase "You have nothing to worry about" is one of those phrases like "Everything will look better in the morning" that is overrated. Kate and I stood in front of the cast list for a full five minutes, stunned by the news. Kate was stunned because she'd been chosen to play the second biggest female role, Anita. I was stunned because I hadn't been chosen to play anything. Oh, officially Mrs. Shale listed me as Jet dancer number four/Velma and Anita's understudy; but Velma only spoke about five words during the entire play, and being an understudy doesn't mean anything. In the entire history of Three Forks drama productions, I've never heard of a main character actually needing their understudy to fill in for them.

Kate, for example, is very healthy, and I could tell by the

way she squealed and jumped up and down in excitement that there was very little chance she would need me to take over for her.

I was going to do nothing in this play but sing backup for some hokey song and do a few twirls and leaps across stage. I suppose Mrs. Shale thought she'd taught me a lesson, and she had. The lesson was: Never trust a drama teacher; they're evil.

Maria went to Mary, and—no surprise—Jordan was Tony. My only consolation was that Lauren had been cast as Shark dancer number three/Rosalia and Maria's understudy. At least she hadn't taken my last boyfriend *and* the part I wanted.

I stared at the list for a moment longer, staring at the main parts on the top of the list and my name on the very bottom. It wasn't worth the time I had to take off from Wal-Mart to perform the part. "I'm not going to be in the play," I finally said. "I quit. Mrs. Shale can find someone else to be Jet dancer number four."

Kate turned away from the list to look at me. "You can't quit. What about all those it's-not-the-size-of-the-part pep talks you gave me?"

"Those were . . ." I didn't finish, because I couldn't think of a way to explain it.

"Those were only for people who should be happy with small parts?" she asked. "Those didn't apply to you, because you're the uncontested star at the school? It's the lead or nothing for you?"

My throat tightened. "Kate, sometimes I think you miss the whole point of friendship. Friendship is not about trying to find a person's faults so you can confront the person with them. Friendship is about saying, 'Yes, it totally sucks that Mrs. Shale made you Jet dancer number four.'"

I headed toward my first period class, and even though I

walked fast, Kate kept pace beside me. "If it had been the other way around and you were Anita and I was some tiny part, I'd still want to be in the play. I didn't quit just because I was a dead person in *Our Town*."

I kept walking.

"Come on," Kate said. "You can help me with my lines. It will be fun."

I'm going to start keeping a list of things people always say but are hardly ever true. After "Things will look better in the morning," and "You have nothing to worry about," the next on the list will be "It will be fun."

It wasn't going to be fun. It was going to be awful. I didn't want to see Lauren and Jordan every day or watch Mary be Maria, and when the crowd cheered on opening night, they wouldn't be cheering for me. But still, I knew Kate wouldn't understand any of that. She'd only remember that when she'd gotten the small part, I'd told her to be satisfied, and when I got the small part, I'd quit. I'd just have to find some way to get through *West Side Story*.

"All right," I said, "I'm officially Velma, Jet dancer number four."

For the first rehearsal we sat on the stage and read the parts out loud so we could get a feel for the story. Jordan showed up—which almost surprised me, since I figured he'd be too mad at Mrs. Shale to be in the play. Maybe she talked with him and smoothed things over. Or maybe he wanted his dad to come down so badly he'd even overlook loose-lipped drama teachers. I tried to find a chance to talk with him, but every other girl in the production flanked him for the entire rehearsal.

The second rehearsal was a little better because at any given time some of the girls had to be onstage learning their blocking, so Jordan was only surrounded by half the girls. He never glanced in my direction. I know because I checked often enough.

During the third rehearsal it became clear that Mary and Lauren were holding a flirting competition. Mary had an edge because she had more stage time with Jordan—and eventually kissing scenes. Still, Lauren was an old pro at man stealing, which made her a serious contender. She took to applying so much lip gloss it looked like her mouth had an oil spill. She wore tops so tight that if you stared hard enough at them, you'd be able to read the washing instructions tags.

Brendan wouldn't be happy if he knew his new girlfriend kept flirting with another guy. I hoped it would get back to him—not so they would break up, but so Brendan would tell Lauren to leave Jordan alone.

That's when I knew I was positively, without a doubt, over Brendan. I wanted him to stay with Lauren.

Jordan didn't actually encourage Lauren and Mary, but he didn't discourage them either. He was friendly to everyone. Well, everyone but me. He treated me like a stranger.

Every day I went home and complained about practice and thus came up with overrated saying number four on my list. Mom kept telling me, "When life gives you lemons, make lemonade." Personally, I would have loved to be at a lemonade stand instead of drama rehearsals, but that wasn't possible. Mrs. Shale had a very strict rehearsal attendance policy. If you missed one rehearsal, she lectured about teamwork and how you had let down the cast. Miss another rehearsal, and your understudy took over.

Velma/Jet dancer number four didn't have an understudy and wasn't in most of the scenes, but I still had to attend the rehearsals anyway. Besides the important role of sashaying across the stage with clenched fists during the first song, I also had to learn Anita's blocking, and to hear any instructions Mrs. Shale gave for the character.

When I was six years old, my cousin tricked me into eating a half a box of bran cereal by telling me a cool prize was hidden in the box. He said I'd find it if I ate enough cereal. Most kids, ones without diabolical relatives that is, couldn't be enticed to eat cereal with the flavor and texture of kindling, even for a toy.

But I did.

Being an understudy is the same sort of thing. All that memorization and time spent at rehearsal is just choking down bran for nothing. I couldn't even wish for some sort of accident to befall Kate so I could step in. Kate was my best friend.

By the second week of practices, I'd learned my dance moves, Anita's part, and Velma's biggest line: "Oo, oo, ooblee-oo." Seriously. She said it four different times. Probably the character was supposed to be drunk, insane, or just really stupid. I wasn't sure which and didn't care enough to try and discover her motivation.

One day after I finished my homework, I was so bored I took Tye, who played Chino, and helped him work on his part. Apparently Mrs. Shale had chosen Tye for the role of a Puerto Rican gang member because he had black hair, not because he had any acting talent. He said each sentence as though it were a question.

"I'll help you run lines," I told him as I took hold of his arm and dragged him to the back of the auditorium. I didn't give him a choice. Guys are just easier to handle when you don't overload them with options.

We worked for ten minutes on speaking with anger, then another five minutes on disgust and defiance. Teasing and flirting seemed an entirely new concept to him, just as it had with Jordan. Which makes me wonder if guys even pay attention to what they're saying when they talk to girls.

"Look, you're in love with Maria," I told him. "It's unrequited love; but you don't know that until you go to tell Maria that Tony has killed Bernardo, and she's more concerned about Tony than her brother. You have to show the audience a devastated man. You need to portray Chino as someone who's capable of killing Tony in the last scene."

He looked at me blankly.

I held out my hand for the script. "Here, let me show you."

I read his lines, adding every bit of desolation I'd felt over the last two weeks and a swagger Brendan always used when he was trying to act tough. Which just goes to show you no relationship is a complete waste of time if you can glean acting material from it.

When I finished, I handed the script back to Tye. "Now you try it."

I didn't know Jordan was standing nearby until he spoke. He'd broken free from his entourage of girls and was on his way out of the auditorium for something. "You're good," he said.

I looked over at him, startled.

"You're a good actress," he added, then pushed the auditorium door open and left.

I watched Tye do an impersonation of my impersonation of Brendan's swagger, but I couldn't concentrate on it. Jordan's words kept replaying in my mind, and even though he'd said them nicely, I knew they weren't a compliment.

For the next few weeks Jordan said nothing to me. Occasionally he looked over in my direction during practice. I figured it was progress. Nothing else interesting happened until Mary had a dentist appointment and missed rehearsal. This meant not only did Lauren get more flirt time with Jordan, she also got up onstage and showed everyone she hadn't memorized Maria's lines. Mrs. Shale then pulled out her standard, even-though-you're-just-an-understudy-you-have-the-responsibility-to-learn-your-lines speech. I'd heard it before. In fact, I'd heard the deluxe version given every year two days before production, punctuated with hysteria because someone in the cast was always still messing up their lines right up until dress rehearsal, and then Mrs. Shale ranted and raved and issued curses on our college applications.

I didn't even put down my history homework while she continued on.

And then Mrs. Shale's voice took on a cold edge. "Jessica, are your lines memorized?"

I set my book down. "Yes."

"Yes, your lines are memorized, or yes, you finally decided to pay attention?"

"My lines are memorized," I said.

She waved a hand at the stage. "Then why don't you come up and show us." Nodding at Kate, she said, "You sit down, and let Jessica show us what an understudy's job is."

I wasn't sure who she was trying to embarrass with this—Lauren or me—but I had a feeling it was me. Still, I climbed up onstage and ran the scene with Lauren. Lauren had to consult the script. I didn't.

When I finished the scene, I walked off the stage, went back over to where I'd sat before, and reopened my history book.

"There you have it," Mrs. Shale said to Lauren. "That's how well an understudy should know her part. If for some reason Mary wasn't able to perform on show night, or if she misses another practice and has to step down from her role, you'll need to be up to speed. Do you understand?"

Lauren smiled happily—too happily for someone who'd just been chewed out—and said, "I'll learn the rest of my lines tonight."

Her cheerfulness didn't make me suspicious. I didn't even put two and two together when Mary didn't show up for the next day's rehearsal.

Mrs. Shale paced around the auditorium for half of practice, shaking her head and mumbling about the irresponsibility of teenagers. When we finished rehearsal, she made the pronouncement: Mary hadn't even had the common courtesy to let anyone know why she wasn't at practice. She must not be serious about the play. The part of Maria now belonged to Lauren.

Which is when I realized that the only thing worse than watching Mary stand in the spotlight, kiss Jordan, and catch Christopher Hunter's attention was seeing Lauren do all of that.

She giggled and clapped her hands together as though she'd just been crowned Miss America.

I'm never going to enter a pageant. I would not be a gracious loser. Instead of hugging the newly crowned winner, I would most likely trip her as she took her victory walk.

And although I didn't trip Lauren, I did send Jordan psychic messages to absolutely, positively not fall in love with her.

The next day when Kate and I walked into the auditorium, Mary stood in front of Mrs. Shale wailing so loudly I could hear her halfway across the room. "I didn't miss practice! You canceled it. You called and left a message with my little brother that you canceled practice yesterday."

Mrs. Shale folded her arms over her black turtleneck sweater. "Mary, we had practice yesterday. Why would I call and tell you otherwise?"

Mary's breaths came out short and close together. Her face turned a mottled red color. "But someone called my house. My brother took the message while I was at the dentist." She waved a hand wildly at Lauren. "It was you, wasn't it? You tricked me into missing practice so you could take my part!"

You'd think after spending the last three weeks in drama rehearsal, Lauren would be able to pull off acting shocked. Instead, she fiddled with her necklace, winding it around one finger. "I did not."

"You did!" Mary shrieked. "It isn't fair." Then in a more desperate tone directed toward Mrs. Shale, she added, "Lauren shouldn't get my part."

Lauren jutted her chin out defiantly. Her voice took on an authoritative tone. "Mrs. Shale already told me I could have it. I spent all night learning my lines."

Mrs. Shale held up her hands and walked between Mary and Lauren, looking back and forth between the two with darting eyes. "Girls, please. We don't need any of this fighting.

Mary, I'm sorry, but you know the rules. It wouldn't be fair to everyone else if I made an exception for you. You missed two rehearsals. Your understudy takes over now, but I'd like you to stay on with the cast as the new understudy for Maria. Can you do that?"

A moment of silence filled the auditorium while Mary clenched and unclenched her fists. "Fine." With her eyes flattened into angry slits, she turned and gave Lauren such an icy glare it would have taken a blowtorch to unthaw it. "You won't get away with this."

Beside me Andre elbowed Tye. "See, I knew sooner or later this play would produce some good drama."

eight

For the next week we had to listen to Lauren constantly humming the tune to "I Feel Pretty." One wouldn't think a hummed song could carry a lot of gloating in it, but Lauren's version did. The pretty-fest may have continued indefinitely if Mary—or rather Mary's father—hadn't put a stop to it. There are apparently many advantages to having a father who is school superintendent, one of which is that he can drop by during school and talk to your drama teacher, and she will actually care about what he has to say. He can assure the drama teacher that his son did in fact receive a phone call stating drama practice had been canceled, and then discuss the ethics of rehearsal rules and the future of the drama program in general.

So after a week Lauren's reign as Maria ended, and Mary stood back on center stage as the prettiest of us all.

Andre started referring to both of them as "the Marias"— as in "Hey, one of you Marias go grab me a soda."

In turn they referred to him as "you jerk"—as in "Go get it yourself, you jerk."

Lauren said snide things to Mary when Mrs. Shale wasn't around, as in "You better not miss any more rehearsals, 'cause

Daddy won't be able to save your part next time." Which had the effect of turning Mary into a paranoid jangle of nerves. She eyed everything Lauren did with suspicion. She waited for the next plot against her. Mary's friends and Lauren's friends stopped talking to each other.

And Jordan still treated me as though he couldn't remember my name.

So all in all we were getting along like any other normal high school group.

The performance dates marched closer on the calendar, and when we weren't onstage, we painted sets or stood with our arms outstretched while Mrs. Shale fitted costumes against our bodies with straight pins.

With only two weeks of rehearsal left, the school newspaper came out with a page-long, anonymous editorial about *West Side Story.* Particularly how our play insulted the Puerto Rican population and promoted violence.

I read the story out loud to Kate at lunchtime, then laid the paper neatly on the table. "What do you think about the article?"

She took a sip from her milk carton. "I think the author has some legitimate points."

I picked up the paper and swatted her with it. "You wrote this, didn't you, Kate?"

"No," she said. "Well, maybe."

I swatted her with the paper again. "Why would you do this? Why would you try to sabotage your own play?"

She scooted her chair out of swatting range. "I'm not trying to sabotage anything. I'm trying to create change. I just pointed out that some people will find the play offensive. It's racist toward Puerto Ricans. It portrays them as gangster thugs."

"It portrays *everyone* as gangster thugs, Kate. It's about two rival gangs."

"Which is another offensive thing. It glorifies violence."

I threw my hands up in the air, giving them something to do besides strangle Kate. "Where in the script does it ever say violence is a good way to solve problems? It shows the damage that comes from violence. Riff, Bernardo, and Tony all die. That's what makes the play a tragedy."

"Right." Kate waved her straw at me as though making a point. "It's too violent for children, and yet you know they'll come and see it anyway. It's needlessly exposing the younger generation to the dark tendencies of humanity. Besides," Kate went on with straw in hand, "even *you* have to acknowledge it's racially insensitive for a drama teacher to fill Puerto Rican parts with white kids."

Kate always uses sophisticated words when her arguments don't carry enough weight by themselves. Usually, I let her get away with it, but not this time. "It's called 'acting' because you pretend to be someone else. None of us are singing, dancing gang members either, but that doesn't mean we can't put on a play."

"I never said we shouldn't put on the play," Kate said hotly. "I just think we should be more sensitive about it."

"Oh, right. We'll be *sensitive* singing, dancing gang members. Instead of racial slurs, we'll insult each other's fashion sense." I picked up the newspaper from the table, glared at the article, then let it fall back down. "Why even be in the play if you feel that way? Why don't you just quit?"

Kate dropped her straw back into her milk carton. "If it takes making that sort of stand—" She stopped talking suddenly, and her gaze shot back over to mine. "You just want me to quit so you can have my part, don't you? That's what this whole conversation is about, isn't it? Well, I'm not going to quit. I can still raise awareness about social injustice while being in the play."

I leaned across the table toward her. "I'm not trying to take your part. I just . . ." The full impact of her words hit me. "Raise social awareness? Kate, what else are you doing?"

She took a bite of her sandwich, and didn't answer me.

"How bad is it?" I asked her.

"It's not bad at all," she said. "I simply sent a copy of my editorial to the *Three Forks News.* They're running a story on it this week."

The *Three Forks News* is one of those free newspapers you don't subscribe to but is thrown on your driveway anyway. It covers events like junior high wrestling and the quilting club. Something as interesting as racial strife in the high school would be front-page stuff.

"Kate, Mrs. Shale and the cast are not going to be happy about this."

She stopped eating. "You're not going to tell them it was me, are you?"

I put my head in my hands. A headache was forming in the part of my brain where the logic is kept. "No, but why can't you ever accept something for what it is instead of stirring up ways to make it wrong? You're a missile-seeking-a-target, Kate."

She humphed and ate the rest of her sandwich in silence. Which was fine with me, since it took all my effort not to rip the newspaper into chunks and pelt her with them.

I worried that the cast would be steamed about the editorial. But at rehearsal those who'd read it just shook their heads and joked about it. "People should really see the play before they judge it," Mary said.

"This is so cool," Andre told Jeff and Tye. "Our very first play is causing controversy. Chicks dig controversial actors."

Kate huffed a lot during practice. I ignored her and sat in the back of the auditorium and did my homework.

Up onstage Andre as Riff, Jeff as Bernardo, and Jordan as Tony ran through the rumble scene. Every once in a while I watched them because I wanted to see their acting methodology, and not because I'm a Jordan groupie who constantly stares at him.

Mrs. Shale stood beside them, correcting their blocking as though teaching waltzing lessons. "Right foot forward, turn, and left arm up higher . . . Timing, people—timing is everything!"

Jeff moved with choppy steps. He didn't look capable of fighting for a parking space, let alone street turf. Mrs. Shale took his place and tried to demonstrate the proper way to stab Andre. She obviously knew a lot about stabbing techniques, since she'd had no compunction about stabbing me in the back.

I doodled a large elaborate *J* on my chemistry notebook. *J* for Jessica. It was most definitely *not* a *J* for Jordan. Jeff stabbed Andre. Then Jordan took the prop knife and stabbed Jeff to complete the scene.

"Much better," Mrs. Shale said with forced cheerfulness. She always spoke cheerfully to Jordan, which lately had gotten on my nerves. I mean, she'd snap at the rest of us for not having enough sparkle as we yelled out street slang, but Jordan could do no wrong.

Mary as Maria, Lauren as Rosalia, and Annabelle—the girl who played Consuelo—came onstage to do the "I Feel Pretty" scene.

I went back to doodling. Next to the *J*, I wrote an *O*. It started out as an *E*, really, but somehow its *O*-ness took over as I drew. Then I added a flowery *R*.

"Hey." Jordan sat down beside me, glancing at my paper as he did.

I put my algebra book over my notebook and blushed. "Hi."

He smiled at me. "Doing homework still?"

"Yeah," I said.

"Which of your classes requires you to doodle my name?"

"I wasn't doodling your name. I'm writing a paper on Jor . . ." I mentally ran through every word I knew that started with a Jor sound—which aren't many. "Ja," I finally finished.

"Georgia?" Jordan asked.

"Yes."

"Georgia doesn't start with *J-O-R*."

"Really? My spelling has always been lousy."

"Your alibis aren't so great either."

I picked up my books and put them behind me. "Did you come over just to criticize me?"

He leaned back, resting his weight against his arms. "No, actually I didn't." Another minute went by. He looked at the stage, and not at me. I waited for him to say something and hoped it would be something I'd want to hear, such as "Sorry I haven't spoken to you for two months," or "By the way, I find the Marias repulsive."

"My father is coming in tomorrow," he said.

"Oh."

"He'll probably show up at rehearsal." Jordan's voice had a sting to it, as though he wasn't entirely happy about this.

"I thought you wanted your father to help you with your acting."

"I do."

Guys. Just when you think you figure them out, they purposely make no sense.

"Do you remember that agreement we made about borrowing your car?" he asked.

"Yeah."

"I'd like to borrow it Friday after school. Will that work for you?"

Would that work for me? He'd ignored me for two months, and then, out of the blue, asked to borrow my car. My pride wanted to tell him what he could do with our agreement—although the fact that he'd just caught me doodling his name sort of let all the air out of any indignation I could muster. Besides, I still wanted to make things right with him. "I guess that would be fine," I said.

He stood up, his eyes on the stage. "Great. I'll talk to you more about it later, okay?"

"Okay," I said.

Then he went onstage to sing a duet with Maria. I tried to go back to my homework, but couldn't think of anything besides Friday and why Jordan wanted to borrow my car.

On Tuesday at rehearsal, I could feel Christopher Hunter's presence as soon as I walked into the room. Instead of lounging around the stage talking, all the kids huddled up front around him. Even kids who weren't in the production mingled with the crowd, smiles animating their faces. Jordan stood beside his father, not speaking, his hands in his pockets.

He couldn't have spoken if he wanted to because everyone else lobbed questions at his father, hung on his responses, and basically stared at him like crazed fans. For the first time I realized how hard it must be to have an idol for a parent, to always be invisible by comparison. More than anything else, this one moment explained to me why Jordan hadn't wanted people to know who his father was. And I'd let them know. It made me feel even worse.

Christopher Hunter looked older than he'd been in his last movie—which shouldn't have surprised me, since the movie came out about three years ago. But it was still a small shock. I'd half expected that his image would remain as unchanged in life as it did on my DVD player. Streaks of gray lightened his hair around his temples, and wrinkles crinkled the corners of his eyes. Still he was a handsome man, an older version of Jordan.

My glance moved to Jordan, and I found him watching me. I stood away from the group, hovering, unsure as to whether I should join them or not. It felt odd to stand all alone, and yet I didn't want to be one more teenager mobbing the movie star. Besides, I wasn't sure if Jordan wanted me there.

I sat down in my usual spot, opened my algebra book, and forced myself to work a problem even though I wanted to look up at Jordan and see if he was still watching me.

Ten minutes past the time we usually started, Mrs. Shale told us to run through the last act. She sat next to Mr. Hunter at the front of the stage, but didn't even try to direct. She turned it over to him. He watched us run through scene after scene and offered advice every few minutes.

Except for the last scene where we were all onstage to help carry off Tony's body in a mournful way, I didn't have anything to do. I sat in the auditorium with the other understudies and miscellaneous fans who'd come in. Lauren sat two seats away from me. I could almost hear her gnashing her teeth together. I tried to do my homework, but every time Jordan's dad stopped the action to tell the actors something, I found myself riveted to his words. He'd done this for real. He actually knew what he was talking about.

I watched him a lot, thinking about all the times I'd seen his name in *People Magazine* articles and TV shows. It's odd to know so much about a person who knows absolutely nothing about you. I wasn't sure how to even address him. In my mind he'd always been Christopher Hunter, but now that he was here in the room, it seemed an impossibly familiar term. He was Mr. Hunter—both of those words being spoken with gilded letters.

Up on stage Jordan spoke most of his lines stiffly, and his father kept stopping him. "You can't act like you're embarrassed to be up there," his father said. "Forget you're on a stage and concentrate on being Tony. If you feel awkward telling Maria you love her, the audience will pick up on that."

Jordan spoke to Mary again, louder but just as stiffly. "We'll be all right. I know it. We're *really* together now."

His father held up a hand to stop the dialogue, then thought better of it and waved at them to continue. "We can work on it at home."

He has done it better, I wanted to say. *He's only nervous because you're here, because you're his father and he knows he can't compete with you in this area.* I didn't say it though. I just pressed my pencil lead down so hard on the paper that it broke.

Finally we did the last scene. I stood onstage with the other gang members, trying to look tough yet somber while the main characters ran their lines. Jordan's father made him die in Mary's arms five times. I was so tired of watching it, I wanted to take the prop gun and shoot myself just so I'd have an excuse to lie down. Then I had to endure Mary waving the gun around at everyone screaming, "YOU ALL KILLED HIM! AND MY BROTHER, AND RIFF! WELL, I CAN KILL TOO BECAUSE NOW I HAVE HATE." It was supposed to be the epiphany of the whole play—the dramatic moment when she threw down the gun, symbolizing hate needed to be thrown away. Only Mary forgot to throw down the gun. She yelled out her lines, then clutched the weapon against her chest and stared out into the audience.

We waited. The guy who played Officer Schrank waited in the wings for her to finish her part so he could come on and say his lines.

Mary glanced offstage and nodded at him.

"The gun," I whispered. "You're supposed to throw down the gun."

Either she didn't hear me or she ignored me, because she still held fast to the gun with one hand and made waving motions to Officer Schrank with the other.

He stood offstage, turned his finger into a gun, and pretended to shoot her.

She cocked her head at him, confused.

"The gun," I whispered again.

Finally, Jordan stood up from the stage, clutching his stomach as though horribly wounded. He staggered over to Mary and held his hand out. "Before I die, I think I have just enough strength to take this gun from you and throw it away."

She handed him the gun, he tossed it on the ground, and then Jordan did a dramatic twirl and fell over dead again.

I clapped for him. Several other cast members joined in.

Mr. Hunter stood up and put both hands on the stage. "Very cute, but that's exactly the sort of thing that can't happen. Look guys, mistakes happen. You have to learn to work around them in a professional way. Jordan, if you had done that during the performance, you would have ruined the whole play."

Jordan sat up on one elbow. "But it's not the performance. It's just a rehearsal."

"And rehearsal is where you learn how to handle the mistakes." Mr. Hunter turned to Officer Schrank. "If Maria forgets to throw down the gun, you just come onstage and say your lines anyway. If anybody forgets anything, you do your best to ad-lib your way out of it and move on. You don't get second chances when you're onstage. Everybody got that?"

Everybody nodded and mumbled yes, except for Jordan and me. He didn't say anything, because he was clenching his jaw too tightly, and I didn't say anything, because I was watching Jordan. He hadn't even wanted to be in this play. I'd made him do it.

"Great." Mr. Hunter clapped his hands together. "I know you'll all do a super job with this play, so I've got some good news for you. I talked to my agent and told him my son was the lead in *West Side Story*. He's coming down to watch the play opening night. I might even get a reporter to show up. Sort of a chip–off–the–old–block human interest story. What do you think of that?"

A chorus of gasps intermixed with excited twitters answered his question. Jordan just stared at him. "Your agent is coming?"

"Yep. He said he wouldn't miss it for the world."

"That's great," Jordan said, but he still needed to work on his acting skills. I could tell he didn't mean a word of it.

nine

The next day at school all anybody talked about was the play, Christopher Hunter, and his agent. Even the teachers wrapped themselves up in the discussion. Everyone wanted to know when tickets would go on sale and how they would be distributed. We'd never sold out a play before, and now it seemed as though the whole town wanted to come just in case—I don't know—the agent held an impromptu talent search during intermission, or something.

As drama class started, the principal strode into the room to talk to Mrs. Shale. He gripped a copy of the *Three Forks News* in one hand. He clenched the other in a fist. Even though the two of them went out into the hallway to talk, the conversation still filtered in to us, partially because they hadn't closed the classroom door and partially because Mr. Poure's voice is loud enough to pierce concrete.

"What kind of play are you putting on?" Mr. Poure asked. "The paper says it promotes racism and violence, and now I hear reporters are coming. We don't need this kind of attention drawn to our school."

Mrs. Shale answered quietly. I only caught a few muffled words, and then Mr. Poure bellowed, "I don't care how many awards it won back in the sixties. We can't have our students calling each other spics and Polacks onstage. What's the news media going to make of that?"

More muffled sounds from Mrs. Shale. Then Mr. Poure again: "Well, you'll just have to change those parts. We can't insult people this way. And change all that gang fighting too. We suspend kids for bringing even toy weapons to school, and now I find out my drama department waves them around every rehearsal. This is a lawsuit just waiting to happen."

More muffled sounds from Mrs. Shale, intermingled with protests about time constraints.

We all sat perfectly still in our seats, staring first at the door and then at each other. "There goes the play," Andre whispered.

"Oh well," Tye agreed. "We still get extra credit for being in the cast."

Mrs. Shale finally came back into the room two shades paler, but she didn't say anything about her conversation with the principal.

I expected she would say something at rehearsal, but she just sat in front of the stage marking up a script while Jordan's dad directed us again.

I had to credit him with having patience. We made as many mistakes as we did the day before, but he didn't seem frustrated at giving us the same instructions over again.

Jordan was a little better. Mary was a little worse. Lauren sat in the audience with her eyes shut and said every line Maria had. When Kate wasn't onstage, I gave her a rundown of everything I'd heard Mr. Poure say. "He wants Mrs. Shale to change the play. Are you happy now?"

"Yes," she said.

Sometimes Kate just misses the point.

After rehearsal ended, Mrs. Shale called us all over and handed out photocopies of the revised script. "I know it's late in the game, but I've had to make some changes to your parts. The principal is worried that some of the scenes and language will be offensive to the audience. You'll need to have your new lines memorized as soon as possible."

Mr. Hunter took one of the scripts from Mrs. Shale's hand and flipped through it. "Did you let the principal know copyright laws prohibit you from changing the text of a play?"

"I did." Her shoulders slumped. "He said when kids are onstage, they forget lines all of the time, and our kids just need to forget all the bad stuff."

"The bad stuff," Mr. Hunter repeated. More flipping. He shook his head and grimaced. "I think I should talk with your principal about this. Perhaps if someone explained to him the nature of the play, he wouldn't be so . . ." Mr. Hunter didn't finish, but I thought of many adjectives to insert in the blank.

"Why don't we go find him right now," Mr. Hunter told Mrs. Shale.

She nodded, and the two of them walked out of the auditorium. The rest of the cast sat down and flipped to our revised parts.

Jeff spoke first. "We're not a gang anymore. We're a group."

Andre shook his head. "We don't call people spics. Now we yell 'nitwit' and 'pizza face' at one another."

I checked my lines and found them unchanged. "I still have to say, 'Oo, oo, ooblee-oo.' That is *so* unfair."

"'Oo, oo, ooblee-oo' isn't offensive," Kate said.

I put down my script. "It is to me." Leaning over, I looked at Kate's script. It was open to the part where the Jet gang— make that "group"—attack her. "Well, I see you're no longer called 'spic' or 'gold tooth.' Now you're 'lying' and 'ugly.' That's got to feel like an improvement."

She pulled her script away from me. "It is."

"Get this," Jordan said. "Mrs. Shale crossed out all the references to Puerto Ricans."

Jeff flipped through his papers. "We're not Puerto Ricans anymore?"

Jordan shook his head. "Nope. Apparently your names are Bernardo, Maria, Chino, and Consuelo for some undisclosed reason."

"That's ridiculous." Jeff threw his script back in his lap. "Since when are the words *Puerto Rican* offensive?"

"Figures," I said. "Maria could have been blond after all."

"How am I going to learn all of these new lines?" Mary wailed. "I've become a victim of political correctness."

"Cracko, jacko," I agreed. "And double Oo, oo, ooblee-oo."

"You can joke about it," Jordan said. "You're not going to be the one up there making a fool of yourself."

"And suddenly I'm really glad of that." I flipped another page of script and sang, "*I feel normal, oh so normal—*"

"It's not going to be that bad," Kate cut me off. "And actually some of this is an improvement because . . ." She didn't finish her sentence. The entire cast turned in unison and glared at her. "Anyway," she went on, "I'd better get home because I have a lot of homework and stuff to do, but I'll see you all tomorrow."

The glares followed her as she stood up and walked out of the door.

Andre turned to me. "Did Kate write that stupid editorial in the paper?"

My cheeks grew hot. I didn't want to rat on my best friend,

but I didn't want to lie either. By next rehearsal Kate might not only admit to authoring the article, chances were she'd defend its contents and call the rest of us insensitive because we didn't agree with her. I looked at my script, and not at Andre. "When the article first came out, I asked Kate if she wrote it and she told me no." Which was true. Of course, she'd fessed up immediately afterward, but technically I wasn't lying.

Jordan tapped his fingers against his plastic armrest. "Did you believe her?"

I didn't answer.

Jeff threw up his hands in disgust. "Oh, man, this is incredible. Our own cast member stabbed us in the back."

"That's politically incorrect language," Andre told him. "I think you should say she pushed us, and we tripped and fell on our own knives, which is what now happens in the fight scene between Riff, Bernardo, and Tony."

"No way," Jordan said.

Andre went back to his script. "Yeah, and we're not rumbling anymore. Now we're meeting to discuss our differences."

Jordan let out a sigh. "Do I still get shot in the end, or does someone just talk me to death?"

Jeff turned another page of his script. "I vote we call a truce between Sharks and Jets and kill off Anita in the first scene."

"She means well," I said.

Mary pursed her lips together. "Yeah. We'll explain that to the audience when they ask why they paid money to see a play about gang violence that contains neither gangs nor violence." She picked up the script and waved it in the air. "Mrs. Shale has ruined the play, and we're all going to look stupid doing it. We'll be humiliated in front of the school, the community, and reporters. I'm going to talk to my father about this."

Andre ran his hand along his armrest. "Mary, wasn't it your father who decided we couldn't display Christmas trees in school buildings?"

"Winter trees," I said. "They banned the word *Christmas* from school."

Lauren snapped her fingers together as though remembering. "And which side of the Should-Huckleberry-Finn-be-taken-out-of-the-library-for-using-offensive-words argument did your father take?"

Mary folded her script and grunted. "Well, it's not like anyone misses that book anyway."

Tye threw up his hands. "We're doomed."

"Maybe my dad will get through to the principal," Jordan said. "Maybe he'll be reasonable about it."

The rest of the cast exchanged looks. None of us had much faith in Mr. Poure's reasonableness, but then again, Jordan's dad was Christopher Hunter. It was entirely possible he could move mountains and still have time left over in the day to walk on water.

We mumbled over a few more indignities, but in the end there was nothing to do but go home. Tomorrow would tell whether we were doing *West Side Story* or some odd farcical play where people said "Daddy-o" and "Riga tiga tum" but got along perfectly fine.

While I gathered up my books Jordan walked over to me. "Can you stay for a minute? I want to talk to you."

"Sure," I said.

The others sauntered out of the room, alone or in pairs. When we were the last ones in the auditorium, Jordan said, "So, about Friday, I've been thinking about it, and I need your help. Well, someone's help anyway. I'll understand if you don't want to get involved in this."

"Involved in what?"

He looked over at the door and lowered his voice. "You know, getting my parents together."

"Oh that. I don't mind helping you." The hurt crept into my voice. "Well, that is if you *trust* me not to mess it up."

He ignored my accusation. "This is the plan. My parents are driving up to the cabin on Friday. I sabotaged a faucet earlier and mentioned to my dad that it didn't work. He still considers himself a plumbing expert from his college days, so he took the bait and volunteered to fix it. He'll drive up with Mom because she has stuff to go through before she can rent it. I won't go along, because I'll be out on a date. They'll have to take my car because I'm going to let the air out of one of my mom's tires before I leave, and I've already asked my dad if I can use his rental car—it's a Jaguar—to impress my date. That would be you, by the way."

"I'm the date?" I asked. "Where are we going?"

"We'll secretly follow them up to the cabin. You'll take your Honda; I'll drive my father's Jaguar."

"And that's supposed to impress me?"

He ignored me. "When my parents park the car and are busy inside, we'll switch my Honda with yours. License plates and everything. When my parents come out, their car won't start because they'll be trying to use my key on your car. They'll be forced to spend hours together."

I waited for him to say something else. He didn't. "How will that get your parents back together?"

He thrust his hands into his jeans pockets and spoke quickly, almost as though trying to convince himself. "They vacationed in that cabin. It's got to have good memories for them. Besides, one of the boxes Mom is going to sort through are the pictures my grandparents took of their wedding day. Grandma gave them to me before she died, and I planted them up there when I unscrewed the faucet. You have no idea how much time I've already put into this. I bought CDs of music they listened to when they were first married, put them by the stereo so they look like they're part of my grandparents' stuff, then took the stereo into an electronics shop and had them disconnect the radio function so my parents can only play CDs. I peppered the entire cabin with high school memorabilia they didn't know my grandparents kept, because my grandparents didn't keep it. I tracked down people who went to the same high school they did and bought some from them."

"You did all of that for your parents?" I had never put that much thought, time, or emotion into anything I'd done for my mom and dad. And now I sort of felt bad for all of those store-bought cards I'd given them on their birthdays. It seemed a shame that Jordan, who cared so much, was likely to get so little from his investment.

"Mom doesn't realize Dad has changed," Jordan went on. "Dad doesn't realize Mom would take him back if he just showed her that he's changed. All they need is time together."

"So what happens when the tow truck takes the car to the shop and they find out their key doesn't actually work the ignition?"

"They won't call a tow truck. They'll think it's the battery—just like when your car wouldn't start—and call me on my cell phone. I'll take a really long time to come up with jumper cables. And when I come up, I'll bring your key with me. That way the car will start, and they'll never figure out what we've done."

A dozen problems with this plan came to mind, still I smiled at Jordan. "I'll do it. But you have to realize we're going to get caught and we're going to get in trouble. They're your parents, so I guess you can decide whether it's worth whatever punishment they dish out. You know them best."

"Your confidence is touching," he said.

"Enjoy driving the Jaguar while you can, because your dad will probably never let you touch it again."

The door to the room swung open, and Jordan's father walked back in. Even from a distance I could tell he was clenching his jaw—which explained where Jordan learned how to handle stress.

"How did it go?" Jordan asked.

"Your principal is an idiot," his father said.

Jordan let out a sigh. "We have to make all those changes?"

"Not all of them. He'll allow you to be a gang and to kill people, but not to yell racial slurs."

I put my hands on my hips. "There is something just wrong about that."

"Don't point that out to him," Jordan said. "You'll make things worse."

After I'd spoken, Mr. Hunter turned his head toward me as though seeing me for the first time. The tension dropped from his face, and he smiled. "You know, I don't think we've ever been formally introduced, but you're Jessica, right?" He held his hand out to me, and I awkwardly shook it.

"Right. And you're Jordan's dad." Of course he was Jordan's dad. He'd been directing us for two days. I'm not sure which flustered me more, that he was famous or that I liked his son.

Mr. Hunter gave a small laugh, probably because he finds people who make no sense amusing, and nodded at me. "So I hear you two are going out this Friday. Have you decided on a movie?"

"Not yet," Jordan said quickly. "We're still talking about it."

"We'd like to see a love story," I added, already asking for mercy. "Or at least something where no one gets incarcerated at the end."

Jordan rolled his eyes at me.

"Love stories can make for great movies," his dad said. "I always enjoyed acting in them."

"That must be where Jordan gets it from then." I'm not sure why I felt the need to defend Jordan's acting skills, but I did. I wanted to say, *Maybe Jordan isn't famous, but every word he utters on that stage is just as important because he's saying them all for you.* It was a shame his dad would never know that. "Jordan does really well portraying the romantic side of Tony," I went on. "I know he's been nervous these last couple of days with you here watching him, but he's really good. Even when it was just the two of us practicing, I could tell he had a lot of talent with the love scenes."

It wasn't until Mr. Hunter raised an eyebrow that I realized what I'd just said. "Not that we were making out or anything," I added.

Jordan winced.

His father raised his eyebrow even further.

I looked at my feet, sort of hoping a big hole would open up and swallow me.

"I see." Mr. Hunter ran a hand over his jaw in a distracted way, his eyebrow now stuck halfway up his forehead. "Well, it's nice to hear he's been . . . uh . . . practicing his part." He then turned to Jordan. "So, are you about ready to head home, or"—a glance at me—"do you still have things to do around here?"

"I'm ready to go home," Jordan said. This meant, *I want to flee from Jessica as quickly as possible.* I didn't blame him. I wanted to flee from me too.

"We'll talk more about Friday later," Jordan said.

"Right," I said. "Great." I picked up my backpack and hurried out of the auditorium as fast as I could.

*P*ractice on Thursday was terrible. No one would speak to Kate except for me, so I was caught in the middle of the glare-fest. Since a lot of the script had changed, no one knew their lines or cues. To make matters worse, Mrs. Shale kept finding things to change or unchange. Mr. Hunter didn't come at all. Jordan said he had a telecon at his hotel about a celebrity fund-raiser, but I figured he just wanted to distance himself from our ill-fated production.

After rehearsal Jordan spent fifteen minutes talking to me about our Friday plans. I was so happy to talk to him—which made me realize how pathetic I was. I mean, if a guy telling you the details of some stupid stunt that's going to get you grounded until graduation can make you happy, there is something wrong with you. This is probably why a lot of people resist falling in love, and why those who don't are doomed to write depressing country music.

Right about then I should have started practicing the guitar.

*O*n Friday, Jordan and I skipped out of school sixth period. I didn't even have to forge a note to get out of drama class. Jordan asked Mrs. Shale if I could help him run his new lines, and she let me go without question.

I was half afraid Jordan's mom would catch him before we even started our trip up to the cabin, but when we rendezvoused at the library parking lot, he told me everything had gone as planned.

He had let the air out of one of his mom's car tires, then did the same to the spare, just in case anyone had thoughts about changing the tire. My parents would have most likely ditched the trip to the cabin and spent the afternoon getting their tire fixed, but Jordan was sure his parents would take care of the cabin first and leave the tire problem until they returned home.

After disabling his mom's car, Jordan put his mom's phone, which he'd surreptitiously stolen earlier, under his Honda's front seat. It was turned on and in the middle of a phone call to my phone, which he now held in his hand. With the mute button pressed on our end, we'd be able to hear any conversation his parents had on the way up; but more importantly, we'd know when they'd left the car and gone into the cabin. This would work perfectly if his parents left when they had told Jordan they were going to leave—at two o'clock—and thus didn't run down the phone's battery before we could sufficiently spy on them.

We were using my phone for this bit of intrigue so Mr. Hunter wouldn't have a problem calling Jordan on his phone when they realized they were stuck at the cabin. Besides, I had the same provider as Jordan's mom, so neither of us would be charged for the call. Jordan assured me his mom wouldn't even notice the extra time on the bill. He talked to his friends in California so much he always racked up a lot of minutes.

I'd already cleaned out my car and loosened my license plate to make it easier to switch. Once that was accomplished, all we would have to do was move Jordan's Pima charm to my rearview mirror, and his parents would never know the difference between the cars—well, assuming they didn't catch us while we switched them, that was.

"Do you have everything you need?" I asked Jordan at the library parking lot.

He nodded toward the Jaguar. "I've got my phone and

yours, a screwdriver, and a flashlight in case they don't leave on time and we have to do this after dark."

"Then we're ready to go."

Jordan took a folded piece of paper from his pocket and handed it to me. "Directions to Ruidoso in case we get separated. But try not to get separated from me. You don't want to get lost up in the mountains on those dirt roads."

I hadn't considered the roads before. "You're taking a Jaguar over dirt roads? Your father is going to kill you."

"Only the last bit is dirt," Jordan said, "and it's for a good cause."

"Right. Sure. I hope your parents aren't the kind that yell at people they hardly know."

Jordan checked his watch. "Let's leave now. We can pull off the road and find some place to wait it out in the mountains. That way we won't have to worry about any unforeseen delays making us miss my parents all together."

I got in my Honda and followed Jordan down the street. As we drove, I tailed him as closely as I dared. If I lost him at a red light, I'd most likely end up wandering around the wrong mountain. I've never been good with directions.

I'm not the type that talks to myself, but during that car ride I did. Mostly I said, "Whatever you do, don't rear-end the Jaguar."

You see, this venture could go wrong in so many ways.

We drove through town and out onto the highway, past the twisted bushes of the desert and slowly up to where the air grew chilly and the forest appeared. We passed two-story pine trees that shrouded the road up the mountainside like an enormous green bower. Finally, Jordan went down a dirt road and pulled off to the side. I parked behind him and walked over to his car, shivering more from the suspense than the cold. Once I slid into the passenger seat, I noticed the phone lay on the dashboard. His parent's voices came through on the speakerphone.

"How close are we to the cabin?" I asked, and then before he had time to answer, "Are your parents almost here?"

"The cabin is about a mile down the main road, and they left twenty minutes after we did. Knowing the way my dad drives, they should be here soon."

I relaxed against the seat. Soft leather caressed my back. I probably didn't have furniture at home as nice as the passenger seat in this car. I let my fingers run over the armrest. "So how are your parents getting along?"

He grunted. "They're mostly just talking about me."

"What's wrong with that?"

He tilted his head at me as though it should be obvious. "It isn't romantic to talk about me."

Not according to most of the girls at Three Forks, but I didn't contradict him.

Jordan waved a hand at the phone. "See, there they go again."

Through the phone we heard his dad say, "What did you use to bribe Jordan into losing his earring?"

"I didn't bribe him with anything," his mom answered. "Believe it or not, he did it to impress a girl at school. It's the same reason his clothes no longer look like hand-me-downs from some heavy metal band that didn't have access to a washing machine. Jessica took him shopping."

Jordan picked up the phone and switched off the speaker function. "We really shouldn't listen to their private conversation."

"They're talking about me. I want to hear it."

He held the phone away. "I don't want you to hear it."

I smiled graciously and held my hand out for the phone. "Well, that's too bad because it's my phone, and if I have to wrestle it out of your hands, one of us might accidentally push the OFF button. Think of that."

His eyes narrowed. "You wouldn't."

"You haven't talked to me for almost two months. I want to hear what your mother has to say about me, besides"—I patted my jacket pocket—"I still have sole ownership of my Civic keys. If you want them, you'll give me the phone."

He glared at me but handed over the phone. "Fine. Have it your way. They're probably finished talking about you anyway."

I pressed the speakerphone button. "Don't you dare do anything to mess up his relationship with Jessica," his mom said—indicating that they weren't finished talking about me.

"He hasn't even said anything to me about her," his dad answered.

"That's probably because he doesn't want you to mess it up."

Jordan reached for the phone, but I held it away from him.

"I didn't do anything to mess up his relationship with Crystal," his dad said.

"*Krista*," his mom said. "And he's never gotten over the embarrassment of that."

Jordan made another attempt to grab the phone, and I had to stretch my hand all the way into the backseat to keep it away from him.

"Jessica is different," his dad said. "She barely talked to me at drama rehearsal, and when she did, she called me Jordan's dad."

His mom laughed for a full five seconds over that, although I couldn't see anything funny about it. Jordan nearly crawled over me to get the phone. As he grabbed it I heard his mother say, "Well, just be careful. I can tell he likes Jessica a lot."

Jordan switched off the speaker. "Okay, we don't need to hear any more of that." He tucked the phone into his jacket pocket, then looked straight ahead, waiting for me to say something. I wanted to ask him if what his mom had said was true, and if it wasn't, why she'd said it. But I was afraid of the answer. Jordan might have lied to her about me as part of his plan to get his parents up to the cabin. Instead, I asked, "So what *was* your most embarrassing moment?"

"Besides now?"

"The embarrassing thing with Krista. What were your parents talking about?"

He didn't answer. He still wouldn't look at me.

"Why did your mother laugh when I called your father 'Jordan's dad'?"

"Because he's probably never been called that before. It's always been the other way around. I've gone through life known as Christopher Hunter's son. He's always been himself. Movie star. Icon. Idol. Whatever." And then Jordan turned to look at me. "You have no idea how much it stinks to have a father who'll always be better-looking and more popular than you."

"He's not better-looking than you," I said. "I mean, Jordan, he's old, and you're way hot."

"Yeah, well Krista didn't think so." He stared at the trees around us again. One of his hands tapped against the steering wheel. "We'd been going out for four months. I spent four months telling my dad how great she was and how perfect we were for each other. I thought we were anyway. I thought she really liked me. So finally on one of his visitation weekends, he met her." Jordan shook his head and didn't say anything else.

"What happened?"

"She made it clear who impressed her more. Right in front of me, she went all crazy and flirty over my dad."

"That is wrong," I said. "I mean, that is like Jerry-Springer-wrong."

He laughed but without much humor. "I haven't introduced him to any girls since then, even though I know it's not his fault." As though he just remembered why we were sitting in the car, he took the phone back out of his pocket and held it to his ear. "It's quiet. Maybe they reached the cabin." He listened for a minute longer. "I don't hear anyone in the car. They must have gone inside." Turning back to me, he held out his hand for my keys. "Okay, it's time for us to do our part."

I pulled my key chain from my pocket. It sat in the palm of my hand in a jumble. "Are you sure we should do this now? In another couple of hours it will be dark. We'd be harder to see."

"But they might leave by then. We need to do this now while we know they're busy."

I dropped the keys in his hand, then zipped my jacket higher. "All right. Let's get this over with."

We left the Jaguar pulled off on the side of the road, got in my Honda, and drove the rest of the way to the cabin. I made Jordan drive my car because I knew we'd be caught. At least one of his parents would hear a car pull up to the house, or happen to look out the window and wonder why another silver Honda Civic sat in the driveway. Worse yet, it was entirely likely that some hot-wiring hoodlum would drive by the Jaguar, see it was unoccupied, and take off with it.

When Jordan's parents started screaming at us, I wanted to pretend I had as little to do with this as possible.

Jordan turned from the main road onto a dirt one that

wound down to a small wooden cabin. He cut the engine and rolled slowly down the drive. Pine needles crunched under the wheels so loudly that every moment I expected to see the door open and one of his parents step out. I gripped the arm-rest and kept my gaze trained on the door.

Jordan eased my Civic next to his own, put the car in park, and slipped my keys into his pocket. "This will just take a minute," he whispered, and was out of the door. I followed him, darting out like a fugitive. Once out in the open, I didn't know what to do. I settled on crouching behind my car while I bit my fingernails.

Jordan retrieved the Pima charm from his car, attached it to my rearview mirror, then knelt behind his car. With a couple of swift twists of the screwdriver, his license plate fell off. He strode over to my car and repeated the procedure. While he switched the plates and screwed them back on, I stared at the house and ruined the remainder of my finger-nails. Four windows faced us. Blinds covered two of them. Curtains were pulled back on the others. Through one of them, I could see movement. Jordan's mother came into view, walking across the room. I didn't breathe. "Your mom," I whispered.

ten

Jordan didn't look up. He just twisted the screws faster.

His mom walked into what must be the kitchen and dropped a box on the counter. Then she stood in front of the window sorting through its contents.

"Is she looking out here?" Jordan whispered.

"Not right now, but she's standing by the window."

He gave the screw a last twist, took my hand, and pulled me over to the back of his Honda. "Okay, now comes the hard part. We've got to get out of here without being heard or seen." Personally, I hadn't thought the easy part had been that easy, and I was not thrilled to hear that what came next would be harder.

Jordan looked over at the cabin. "My mom can't be standing there when we start the engine. She'll hear us and look up."

"So you want to wait here until she moves?"

"We can't wait. She might glance out the window and see two cars."

We stared at one another. I tried to think of something to help instead of reminding him that I'd told him this would never work. "Call the cabin," I said. "If the phone rings, she'll go answer it."

Jordan dug his phone out of his pants pocket. While we squatted behind the car he punched several buttons. After a moment Jordan's mom turned away from the counter and walked out of sight. As soon as she did, we both scurried around the sides of Jordan's car and climbed in. I slid down in my seat to be less visible. Jordan slipped his key into the ignition, but didn't turn it. "Hi Mom, did you make it up to the cabin?" A pause. "Great." Another pause. "No, nothing's wrong. I'm just whispering because I'm . . . in the movie theater." Another pause. "Jessica and I decided to hit a matinee before dinner." Using his free hand, Jordan snapped his safety belt in place. "I was just wondering, does the CD player at the cabin work?" Jordan put his hands on the key, ready to start the ignition. "I want to know just in case I ever decide to hang out there before you rent out the place." Another pause. "Can you check just to make sure? And turn it up loud to make sure that the speakers work okay too." A longer pause. "Humor me, Mom. I'm the only offspring you have."

As soon as Jordan heard music coming from the phone, he turned the car on and backed up the drive. It seemed loud. The engine, the pine needles, his voice. I wasn't sure the stereo inside the cabin would be noisy enough to drown it all out. I also wasn't sure that Jordan—driving one-handed, quickly, and backward—was going to make it to the main road without taking out a few pine trees or bushes along the way.

But neither happened.

After our car pulled onto the main road, Jordan told his mom, "Thanks, I gotta go now. The movie is about to start," and hung up. Two minutes later we parked beside the Jaguar. He turned to me with a grin. "See, the whole thing was simple."

"That wasn't simple," I told him. "Look at my fingernails."

"Now if switching the Hondas back after this is over proves just as easy . . ."

"I'll have nothing on the end of my fingers except for bloody nubs."

"You worry too much." He sent a contented sigh in the direction of the cabin. "Well, I guess we can split up and drive home. Do you want to come back with me when my parents call for a jump start? If it's too much of a hassle, I'll tell them I dropped you off at home before I came up."

"It's no hassle," I said a bit too quickly, and then added, "I mean, I'm the loyal type of girlfriend who doesn't bail out on dates just because car maintenance is suddenly involved." I knew in a moment he would leave to drive the Jaguar, and I'd have to drive his Honda home. I wanted to spend more time with him. I looked at my hands instead of his eyes, just in case he could read my mind.

Jordan took my keys from his pocket, twisted my Honda key off of the chain so he could start my car when he went up to help his parents, then handed the rest of my keys to me. "When I come back up for the jump start, I'll tell my dad to drive the Jaguar home. That way I can drive your Civic to your house so we can switch our cars again. See how simple it will be? Your fingernails will be spared."

"What if they realize it's not the battery and just call a tow truck?"

"Then you'll have to go into the auto mechanic's and cause a distraction while I swap the cars. Or the keys. Whichever is easiest."

"And just how am I supposed to cause a distraction?"

He shrugged. "You're the actress. It should be easy for you.

Consider it your first real acting job. You can flirt with the mechanic."

"Flirt with the mechanic? Jordan, have you ever gotten a good look at a mechanic? They're all, like, old greasy guys named Gus."

He opened the car door, letting in a blast of cool air mingled with pine scent. "Yeah, but you can flirt with people you don't like if it means getting something you want. After all, that's what you did with me."

The accusation hit me like a slap. My head jerked back, and I gasped out, "I did not."

He lifted an eyebrow in a gesture of disbelief.

"Jordan, my feelings for you were real."

"Then it's too bad they weren't strong enough to keep you from trading me in for a part in the play."

I wanted to reach over and grab him, to keep him in the car with me until he understood. Instead, he climbed out. "That isn't fair," I called after him. "I didn't know Mrs. Shale would tell everyone."

He turned around, tilting his head down to look at me. "Which is why the point of keeping a secret is that you don't tell anyone." He looked over at the Jaguar and shrugged as though he'd grown tired of the conversation. "It's okay, Jessica. I understand why you did it. I understand because my dad used to be the same type of person. He loved acting so much that he traded his family in for all the fame. I don't blame you for wanting to be a star. I'm sure you have the talent and the drive to make it. I'm just tired of being traded." He turned and walked over to the Jaguar.

"It wasn't that way," I called after him, but I'm not sure he heard me.

With a shaky hand I shut the door, then started Jordan's Honda. I hadn't traded him. I'd just made a mistake. Couldn't he find even an ounce of forgiveness for me? I wasn't his father. I didn't want fame more than anything else. I didn't.

As I put the car in gear I thought of the daydreams I'd nurtured over the last few years. I saw myself on the screen, at a movie premiere, lounging by the pool, walking down a red carpet, and through all of it, I was alone.

The Jaguar pulled onto the street ahead of me. I eased over the dirt and back to the road so I could follow him. This time the sound of crushed pine needles sounded like hundreds of little pieces of my heart.

On the way home I didn't tail Jordan closely. I didn't want him to see my face in his rearview mirror. It's bad enough to try and drive while tears keep blurring your vision, I didn't want him to witness the whole event. Besides, by the time we made it to the highway, I knew how to get home on my own. I let the Jaguar pull so far ahead of me I didn't see it anymore.

I regretted telling Jordan I'd go back to the cabin with him. The last thing in the world I wanted was to be stuck in a car with him. An hour of trapped silence up to the mountain, and then another hour coming back. I almost called Jordan and told him I'd changed my mind, but I decided against it. What was the point of making myself look childish? Christopher Hunter wasn't going to call his son when he had car problems. He'd call a tow truck.

At six my phone rang. "I just got the call from my dad," Jordan told me. "I'll be by to pick you up in a half an hour."

It was fifty minutes later that he rang the doorbell. Which in guy-time is only a little late. "I stopped by the Texaco station to fill up a gas can for my parents," he told me with a half smile. "Just in case that's the problem."

I followed Jordan out to the Jaguar. As I slid into the passenger's side I glanced into the backseat. "So where's the gas can?"

"Well protected in the trunk. My father would probably rather walk home from the cabin than have me spill gasoline inside a Jaguar."

I could think of nothing else to say. Well, nothing except for a treatise on how telling your drama teacher a guy's true identity in order to get a play funded is not trading him in for a part in a play. Only I needed to think of a better way to put it because said like that, it sort of did sound like I traded him in for a part in a play.

Which I hadn't.

Jordan pulled into the street and headed into town.

"When your parents called, did they sound like they were getting along?" I asked.

"It's hard to say, but they're through fixing things and sorting stuff, so they'll have to talk until we get there. There's nothing else to do. The place doesn't even have a TV. With any luck she'll be calling him Kit by the time we get there."

"Kit?"

"The nickname she uses for him when she's feeling happy, nostalgic, or has just finished one of her Christopher Hunter movie marathons. The rest of the time she calls him 'your father'."

"Oh."

We drove through Three Forks and out onto the highway. I did a lot of armrest tapping and looking out the window.

Jordan tuned the radio to an oldies station and sang along to a Beach Boys tune.

How can guys be so clueless to the stress level in their environment?

"Twist and Shout" came on. He sang along to that one too. Halfway through "Blue Suede Shoes," I leaned over and turned down the radio.

"I didn't trade you in," I said. "I made a mistake. I let your secret slip out while I was talking to Mrs. Shale, but I didn't think she'd tell everyone about it."

He shrugged. "So the moral of the story is: Don't trust people who value drama over keeping their word?"

"Yes," I said, and then just as quickly, "No, because you're about to say that applies to me too."

"Doesn't it?"

"No. There are lots of things more important to me than drama."

"Name some."

"My family. My friends. My values. Eating." A long pause in which I tried to think of something else to add to the list. "Air."

"Too bad I didn't make the list," he said.

"You did. I thought you were a friend. But I guess we were both wrong." I went back to looking out the window, and after that, neither of us said anything else.

We pulled up to the cabin and parked the Jaguar adjacent to my Honda. Jordan's dad was sitting on the steps underneath the porch light reading a magazine. His mom was nowhere around. I didn't take this as a good sign that anything romantic had transpired between them.

Mr. Hunter stood up as we got out of the car. "Thank goodness you're here. My joints are all starting to freeze together."

Jordan walked around to the back of the Jaguar and opened the trunk. "Why didn't you wait inside?"

"Because there are colder things inside. Namely your mother."

Jordan picked up the jumper cables, then held them limply in one hand. "You and Mom have been fighting?"

Mr. Hunter flipped the hood of the Jaguar up, then went around to the driver's side and turned the car on. He took the cables out of Jordan's hands and strode over to the Honda. "Sorry, Jordan. I shouldn't have said that about your mother. It's just this stupid cabin. It's brought back all the old memories—and apparently I was a villain in every one of them."

Jordan leaned up against the Jaguar and watched his father connect the cables to the Honda's battery. "You don't have any good memories of the cabin?"

"Well, I did until tonight."

Jordan's mom walked out of the front door. She folded her arms when she saw us. "There you are. It's eight thirty. I nearly called the police to see if you'd been attacked by wild bears on the way up."

"Uh, sorry, Mom," Jordan said. "I got a gas can in case that was the problem, then I had to drive slow so none of it would spill."

She trudged down the steps. "Well, let's get on with this and see if the car will work."

Mr. Hunter walked toward the front seat of the Honda, but Jordan beat him there. He plopped into the driver's seat. "I've got it, Dad." Mr. Hunter returned to the Jaguar, sat in the front seat, and revved the engine.

I stood in front of my car because I didn't know where else to go. Jordan's mom walked up beside me. "I'm really sorry to ruin your date this way," she said with forced cheerfulness. "But what can I say? It's not like you plan for these things to happen."

Well, not unless you're Jordan anyway.

I nodded at her. "It's fine." Or at least I hoped it would be once my car started.

Mr. Hunter gave Jordan the signal to start his engine. He tried. The car made a whining sound, but didn't start.

"Try it again," Mr. Hunter said, and gunned the Jaguar harder.

My Civic made another sound, this time with more grinding and less whining, but it still didn't start.

I saw Jordan's look of dismay through the windshield. "It's not working," he said.

I stepped over to him. "Try speaking to it gently."

Jordan didn't say anything, but he turned the key again. It only clicked this time.

I leaned against the car and tilted my head in the driver's side window. "Try telling it that it's a good car—oh, and if that doesn't work, threaten to push it over a cliff."

He turned the key again and got another click for his efforts.

Mr. Hunter turned off the Jaguar and strode over to the rest of us. "I don't think it's the battery after all. That sounded like the starter motor. Have you had trouble like this before?"

Jordan's gaze darted to mine, then back to his father's. "Now that I think of it, there have been a couple of times when it didn't start right off."

Mr. Hunter shook his head and put his hands on his hips. "This is what comes from purchasing cheap cars. I'll buy you something decent when we get back to town. What kind of car do you want?"

Jordan turned the key again. *Click.* "You don't have to do that, Dad."

"I want to," Mr. Hunter said. "How about a Lexus? They're reliable."

Jordan's mom narrowed her eyes at her ex-husband. "This is just like you. You think every problem can be solved by throwing money at it."

"Every problem—no. Car problems—yes."

She folded her arms. "Jordan doesn't need a new car. We can get the starter motor fixed."

Mr. Hunter matched her stance, putting his hands on his hips. "And then something else will fall apart. Do you think you're the only one that worries about Jordan's safety? He needs a new car."

"Then I'll buy it," she said.

When my parents fight, they raise their voices. Jordan's parents lowered theirs. "You don't want to buy him a car," Mr. Hunter said. "You're just determined not to let me have any part in his life, aren't you?"

"Oh, that's rich coming from you. Where have you been for the last seventeen years?"

Jordan flung the door of the Civic open. "Stop it!" he yelled. "I can't believe the two of you can't get along for one evening. I can't believe this!" He slammed the door, then stormed up the cabin steps. One slam later he was inside.

Jordan's mom and dad looked at each other. Then they looked at me.

I had been on some bad dates in my life, but this one outdistanced them all. There is nothing more awkward than being stuck at a cabin with two arguing adults and their son who no longer likes you. The silence felt colder than the night air.

Finally, Mr. Hunter's gaze turned back to his ex-wife. "I'm sorry," he muttered.

Ms. Hunter looked at the ground. "No, it was my fault. I just . . ." She sighed, put one hand to her temple like she had a headache, and then looked over at the cabin. "We'd better go in and talk to him."

"Right," Mr. Hunter said. Then without another glance at me, they walked up the steps. Together, but stiffly apart.

With my hands in my pockets, I stared at the cabin. What exactly was a girl who was pretending to be a guy's date supposed to do in the middle of a family fight? I'm not sure Miss Manners has ever covered this topic in her etiquette column.

Finally—mostly because I didn't want to go inside—I decided to try my Civic again. Jordan had left my key in the ignition, so I just slid into the car and patted the steering column. "There, there, you're a good car." I turned the key. Nothing. "All right then, you're an awful car. If you had started when you were supposed to, everything would have been fine—but no, you had to turn this event into something truly horrible because you're an evil, evil car."

I smacked the steering column just to emphasize the point.

The next time Kate tells me about my charmed life, I'm going to give her a quick reality check by referring to this moment. I'd told my father for ages that my Civic was a piece of junk, and the only thing I ever got for my trouble was a lecture on the cost of car payments. Jordan's car didn't start once, and two seconds later his parents were arguing over who got to buy him a new one.

I wondered if he would fess up that it was my car that didn't work or whether he'd just let them buy him a Lexus. And if so, what would happen to my car? His parents would most likely fix the starter motor so they could trade it in—and wait—didn't car dealers check the serial numbers on vehicles against the owner's registration? They must. When Jordan's parents tried to trade in my Civic, we'd be caught.

I smacked the steering column again. "This could have gone perfectly smoothly, and now I'm going to be stuck flirting with some greasy mechanic named Gus."

I sat glaring at my car for another five minutes, and then because I'm an optimist, I tried the key again. This time it worked. I nearly cried out in joy. Letting the car idle, I ran up to the cabin, opened the door, and called out, "Um, excuse me, I got the Honda to start."

One by one Jordan and his parents emerged from the living room. Most of the tension had left the group. Jordan's face was devoid of emotion, but his parents did their best to act happy.

"Great," his mom said. "That will save us a call to a tow truck."

"We'll stick together on the drive home to make sure it doesn't have any more problems," his dad added.

Jordan shrugged listlessly and walked back outside. "Fine."

Mr. Hunter watched him go, and then turned to me. "Hey, I'm sorry Jordan had to come up here and ruin your date and all. I'll make it up to you kids though. I'll make reservations in the nicest restaurant in town for you tomorrow night, okay?"

"You don't have to," I said. "Really." Because first of all, this would not make Jordan happier; second of all, it feels horrible to have someone apologize to you for something that is actually your fault; and last, the nicest restaurant in Three Forks is Applebee's, and you usually don't need reservations to go there. I slipped out of the door and hurried to catch up to Jordan. His mom must have said something to his dad because behind me I heard Mr. Hunter say, "Making a reservation at a restaurant is *not* throwing money around."

Jordan climbed into the Honda. His father came and stood next to the driver's side window. "Don't you want to drive the Jaguar home?"

"No," Jordan said, "I want to take a farewell ride in my Honda."

Mr. Hunter smiled. "All right. Just make sure you don't turn the engine off when you take Jessica home, or you might be stranded at her house."

"Okay," Jordan said. He didn't look at his father.

"We'll follow you back to Three Forks." Mr. Hunter tapped the car door with his hand as though giving it his blessing, and then walked over to the Jaguar.

I didn't know what to say, so I didn't say anything as I got into the car.

Jordan pulled out onto the dirt driveway and drove silently back to the main road. Finally, when we were halfway down the mountain, he glanced over at me. "So, were you waiting for a sign from God before you got your car fixed? Because if so, this was it."

"I'll tell my father it wouldn't start again," I said. "But unlike your father, he seems more concerned about his wallet than about his child having reliable transportation."

"Well, I guess that's one more reason for you to be a movie star then. After you make it in Hollywood, you can buy off your children with new cars."

"Your dad was just trying to be nice to you," I said.

"If he wanted to be nice to me, he never would have left the family in the first place," Jordan flung back.

Sometimes people show you wounds too big to be healed

with words. I wished I knew a magic phrase to make all his pain go away, but I didn't. I wasn't even sure what the right trite phrase to say was. We drove on, the quiet growing so big it seemed suffocating. "I'm sorry tonight didn't go the way you wanted it to," I said.

He nodded, and didn't speak. His knuckles were white against the steering wheel. His jaw muscles pulsed. We left the mountainside, and drove onto the highway. The silence stretched on like the road before us. Jordan was miserable, and I hated sitting there saying nothing.

"Maybe they're just happier without each other," I said. "You want them to be happy, don't you?"

Jordan rolled his eyes. "My dad still has family pictures from ten years ago hanging up in his house. My mom never goes out with anybody past the third date. He sends me money on her birthday so I can buy her something nice. She has every one of his movies and every episode of his police show. She says they're for me, but I'm not the one who'll go on doughnut binges and watch episode after episode at midnight. The first thing he always asks me when I come for a visit is how my mom is. She still has her wedding dress stashed in a box in her closet. Why would a woman whose only child is a son keep her wedding dress?"

Well, if it were my family, the answer would be that my mom wanted to get remarried and was too thrifty to buy a new wedding dress. But somehow I doubted this was the case for Jordan's mom.

Jordan shook his head. "They just can't let go of the little things long enough to grasp what would make them happy." He let out a grunt of disgust. "I don't know why I even tried to help them. If they want to live miserable, lonely lives, there's nothing I can do to stop them."

The only conversation for the rest of the car trip came from the radio. It was clear Jordan didn't want to talk, and after a few more attempts, I gave up and just stared out the window into the darkness.

When we pulled up at my house, Jordan turned off my car, took the screwdriver from his jacket, and switched the license plate from my car to his. Then he screwed my plate back on. "Well, your debt to me is paid."

"Right." The word sounded hollow in my throat. "I guess I'll see you at drama practice."

"Let me walk you to your door."

We made our way silently to my door. It seemed strange he was saying good-bye this way, since ours had never been a real date. Usually, when I said good night to a guy on the doorstep, I told him what a good time I'd had. I didn't know what to say now.

When we got to my front door, Jordan checked his watch. I knew it was about ten o'clock since staring at the car clock had been one of the few activities available to me on the ride home. "Are your parents still up?" he asked me.

"Probably."

"Do you want me to go talk to your dad about the starter motor on your car?"

"That's okay. I'll tell him."

Jordan looked at the door, then back at me. "You told him before, and he didn't fix it. The problem will just get worse, and if you don't take care of it, you really will be stranded someplace."

"I'll tell him."

"Is it the money? I can loan you the money if you need it."

I put my hand on the doorknob, but didn't open it. "My parents aren't destitute, Jordan. They're just cheap. And busy.

And, well, they're sort of procrastinators too, but they can get the car fixed."

"Right away?" he asked. "When you were stuck at Wal-Mart, you didn't even have your phone with you, Jessica. What are you going to do if you get stranded out in the wilderness somewhere?"

"I don't usually drive my car out into the wilderness and then turn off the engine, Jordan."

He waved a finger at me. "See. I can tell you're not taking this seriously. I'm talking to your dad."

And then he did. Jordan walked into my house, found my dad paying bills at the kitchen table, and told him my starter motor needed to be replaced.

My dad acted all surprised about this, like it was the first time he'd ever heard about it, or maybe he was just surprised that Jordan had come inside to tell him about it. But at any rate, Dad promised he'd look into it tomorrow.

Then I walked Jordan back to the door, blushing, though I'm not sure why. I guess it was partly because Jordan had sort of called my dad on the carpet for not fixing my car, but mostly it was because I'd just realized Jordan still liked me.

This moment was like the family pictures hanging in Christopher Hunter's house. It was an old wedding dress stashed in the closet. Jordan wanted to make sure I was safe in my car.

"See you at rehearsal," he told me.

"Definitely," I said.

eleven

Over the weekend I thought of all sorts of things to talk to Jordan about—questions to ask, ways to comfort him. On Monday and Tuesday at rehearsal I never had a chance to say any of it. We were practicing with the orchestra for the first time, which meant Mrs. Shale made Jordan run through all his songs about ten times. When he wasn't belting out "Something's Coming" or "There's a Place for Us," Andre, Tye, and Jeff surrounded him. They came up with secret gang handshakes. And no, this wasn't in the play—this is just how guys amuse themselves when they have too much time on their hands.

Mr. Hunter didn't come. Jordan told the cast his dad had some business to take care of in California, but would be back opening night. Which I suppose meant his parents hadn't reconciled on the way home from the cabin.

On Wednesday at dress rehearsal, almost everyone ran around in nervous disorganization. When Jordan wasn't onstage, he stood in the wings with the rest of the cast to see how we managed our first live run-through.

As it turned out, we didn't manage it very well. The new lines still messed up some of the cast, who either forgot to change them or forgot what the new version was. As a protest to the new politically correct rendition of the play, Andre said all of his lines as though his character, Riff, was psychotic. He made the phrases "Riga tiga tum tum" and "Daddy-o" sound like something you could be arrested for.

We finished our Jet dance four beats after the music stopped. Jordan dropped the knife when he was supposed to stab Jeff, so Jeff just stood there waiting for Jordan to pick up the knife and kill him. The Sharks and the Jets both broke out laughing until Mrs. Shale stood up to yell her You-are-not-taking-this-seriously speech. We'd heard this tirade along with her Timing-is-everything! outbursts in increasing intervals throughout the week, and I knew her near-nervous-breakdown screaming fit loomed just around the corner.

The light crew apparently had some difficulties because every once in a while the stage lights would disappear, and then we'd stumble around in the dark saying our lines blindly while we tried not to bump into the sets. Half the time the spotlight trailed after whomever it was supposed to illuminate, so it looked like a huge white dot was chasing the characters.

Then in the second act when Anita is supposed to push open Maria's bedroom door, the door came off its hinges and toppled over. If Mary hadn't jumped away, it would have flattened her. Instead of going on with the scene, Mary stormed to the edge of the stage and waved a hand wildly in Lauren's direction. "See, Mrs. Shale! Lauren is trying to kill me to get my part. Now you have proof. She rigged that door!"

Mrs. Shale tapped her pencil against her script and called backstage, "Someone from props crew get the door off the set!" She then turned to Mary. "Accidents happen. No one is trying to kill you. We'll make sure it's fixed for tomorrow's performance." Waving a pencil at Mary, she collapsed back onto her chair. "Continue on."

Mary put her hands on her hips. "Doors don't just fall over!"

For two seconds Mrs. Shale said nothing. Then she stood up, heaving deep breaths while her face reddened. She flung her script down on the chair and yelled, "I don't care if the whole set falls down! I don't care if you forget your lines, your props, or your dance moves. I don't care if you develop a full-blown case of amnesia! When you run through a play, you don't stop in the middle of a scene. Ever! Now continue on!"

Evidently the near nervous breakdown had arrived.

Mary went on and recited her lines sullenly, which matched Kate's performance, since she'd been sullen ever since the rest of the cast stopped talking to her.

Finally rehearsal ended, and Mrs. Shale gave us the usual half pep talk/half threat speech. She told us in drama tradition, a bad dress rehearsal meant a good opening night, and after today we were bound to have a great performance tomorrow night.

But I'm not sure she meant it. I noticed she'd nearly chewed through her pencil.

Jordan left before I could say anything to him, which really annoyed me. I mean, he liked me. I knew it, and yet he still wouldn't talk to me long enough to work things out. And then he had the nerve to be mad at his parents for doing the same thing. What kind of justice was that? I needed to talk to him while we were both still in the play and I at least had a chance to be alone with him. If I could ever get a chance to be alone with him again.

*A*t five o clock on Thursday, we all showed up at the auditorium to get into our costumes and run over trouble spots before the performance started. We went through the opening Jet dance until we ended at the same time the music did. Jordan stabbed Jeff so many times that Jeff nearly died before Jordan even pulled his knife out. The spotlight stopped chasing the actors and illuminated them instead. Mrs. Shale finally quit smacking things with her fists while she talked to us. She still mumbled out, "Timing is everything," once in a while, but even this mantra had taken on a resigned tone.

Then we went to the greenroom and waited for the auditorium to fill up. Lauren brought us all gingerbread man cookies shaped like our characters, which even I had to admit was way creative. Mine had long blond hair frosting. Jordan's wore a bandanna to make him look like a tough-guy gang member. Andre made a big deal because his gingerbread man cookie was lighter colored than some of the others. "Is that some sort of racial slur? Are you insulting my Latvian heritage?" He waved the cookie in Kate's direction. "I'd better run this past the mistress of political correctness."

"Shut up and eat your cookie," I told him.

"Or you can just give it to Mrs. Shale," Jeff added. "She's ready to bite your head off anyway."

Kate nibbled away at her Anita cookie. "One day you'll thank me for making you aware of all the social oppression around us."

"Kate," I said, "shut up and eat your cookie."

After Lauren put the Maria cookie in her hand, Mary eyed it suspiciously. "Thanks, did you add any *special* ingredients to mine?"

Lauren's expression twisted in disgust. "Sorry, I didn't have any ingredients to boost your acting skills. So you'll still give a lousy performance."

Mary turned the cookie over in her hands. "This is probably laced with ex-lax, isn't it?"

"You're such an ungrateful pig," Lauren answered.

Kate walked over to them and held out her hands, pleading. "You guys, this is not the time to fight. We're trying to deliver a message of peace to the audience. How can we do that if we can't find peace together, right now?"

Mary pursed her lips. Her fingers tightened around her cookie until I thought she'd crush it. "I don't care what message I'm delivering, I don't trust Lauren." She handed the gingerbread man to Kate. "But if you want to trust her, by all means, go ahead and eat my cookie too."

"We need to get along," Kate said, but by that time Mary and Lauren had both turned and walked off. Still, Kate bit off one leg and than the other of the Maria cookie. As she gnawed on the middle she leaned up against the counter by me. "Man, I can hardly wait until this play is over. It's nothing but stress and more stress. My stomach has been doing backflips since dress rehearsal."

"You'll do fine," I told her.

"Andre is never going to stop with his political correctness cracks."

"Eventually he'll find something else to occupy his attention."

Tye, who'd gone out to check on the size of the crowd, ran back into the greenroom. "The place is packed, and guess what—there isn't just one news camera in the auditorium, there are three. They're taking turns interviewing Jordan's dad and Mrs. Shale."

A chorus of squeals went up from the girls in the room. Jordan, who stood in front of the costume rack reciting lines, suddenly began spitting them out like he was being interrogated by the play-police.

"I don't want to do this in front of reporters," Kate said. "I feel sick."

"You'll be fine." I patted her shoulder. "The whole thing will be fine."

Which just goes to show you that I'd make a lousy fortune-teller.

*P*ersonally, I wasn't even nervous when the curtains came up. I mean, I'm used to having main parts in plays, so being a background dancer isn't enough to rattle me. And as for my part as Velma—with lines like "Oo, oo, ooblee-oo"—who would be able to tell if I screwed it up? Plus, my parents never came till closing night, so I didn't have to think about them watching me from the audience.

I wasn't even flustered when half the Jet dancers finished the opening dance two measures ahead of the song, making the rest of us look like we were behind. Big deal. What self-respecting gang members have rhythm anyway? It's hard to count the beats to songs with all that cracko-jacko they're doing.

But the cameras seemed to have a bad effect on everyone, and as the play went on, the mistakes increased. Jeff delivered all of his lines in a rush, as though he couldn't wait to get them out of his mouth. Kate said hers like she was in pain.

Annabelle tripped during the "I Like to Be in America" dance number and just barely saved herself from falling into the orchestra pit. With one of her legs flailing, she took out a clarinet player, which sort of ruined the continuity of the song.

The gang members kept forgetting their cues, and they

either skipped big chunks of dialogue or had breaks where they just stood around not knowing who was supposed to speak next. In those parts Andre always improvised in a horrible way.

When the actor who played A-rab forgot his, "Where you gonna find Bernardo?" line, Andre struck an Elvis-like pose, then said, "So you Jets want to sit here shooting the breeze, or do ya wanna do something fun like holding up a Circle K?"

The other cast members stared at him blankly.

"We're hoodlums, so we should do hoodlum things. You know, rob convenience stores, trip roller skaters, and let dogs out of peoples backyards. Or, hey, I know, *we could find Bernardo at the dance tonight at the gym.* How about that, A-rab?"

"Great, Daddy-o," A-rab said.

"And great Mommy-o too," Andre replied.

Which just goes to show you some people can't be trusted in front of a camera.

During the scene where the gang members yell insults and then set up the rumble, instead of saying the revised line, "Jerk!" one of the Jet gang yelled out, "Spic!" then clapped his hand over his mouth like he'd just been caught cursing at a church service. He looked helplessly toward the camera and said, "I didn't mean that."

Andre smiled stiffly at the rival gang. "Yes he did. He meant that insult and many more! We curse you Sharks and all your Sharky spawn!"

"Idiot!" One of the Sharks yelled back, but it was uncertain whether he was speaking to Andre or his character because he said the line with a smirk.

"Wop!" A Jet yelled in return, and then winced at his mistake. "I mean, Whopper! That's right. You're nothing but a big burger who's growing stale in some fast-food joint!"

"We accept!" Jeff shouted, which didn't really make sense anymore.

Backstage the Jet girls all planned on dumping our gang boyfriends so we didn't have to be seen with them in tomorrow's performance.

From the wings Mrs. Shale shook her head, grasped her shirt with one hand, and muttered, "Oh, oh, oh!" as though she was being struck with something.

Right before our eyes *West Side Story* became a comedy. I wondered if the scriptwriters were alive and if they could sue us for defaming their musical.

Only Jordan managed to keep any dignity during all of this. He said his lines flawlessly. Thoughtfully. Unfortunately, he almost looked odd doing it that way, since the rest of the cast was falling apart around him. Still, when he rammed the prop knife into Jeff, his anger seemed real, and when he stood over Jeff's prone body and cried out, "Maria!" I wanted to cheer for him.

During intermission Mrs. Shale gave us a talk that would have rivaled those given in the locker room during the Super Bowl. Our whole lives would be affected—no, *apexed*—by whether we could pull our acts together and stop humiliating her as a drama teacher. After she delivered her speech, she marched out of the greenroom to let us "think about it."

Like that was going to suddenly change everything. Like "apexed" was even a real word. As soon as she left, half the cast raided the soda machine. Andre, Tye, and Jeff drank their root beers without stopping for a breath, and then tried to burp to the tune of "I Feel Pretty."

I bought two Diet Sprites and brought one to Kate. She set it down on the makeup counter without opening it, then wrapped her hands around her stomach and slumped into a chair. "I feel sick."

I patted her on the shoulder. "You're doing great, Kate. You knocked 'em dead with that last song."

"Yeah, well, death would explain their lack of applause."

"They clapped," I said. Maybe not a lot, maybe not vigorously, but still there had been definite hand motion going on.

She leaned her head against the chair. "I don't think I can go back out there."

"Yes, you can. You can do it."

Kate gave a small whimper, then leaned forward and threw up on the floor.

"Okay," I said. "Maybe you can't do it."

Kate shot up out of her chair and ran out of the room with her hand covering her mouth. I stared bleakly at the mess and hoped she made it to the bathroom in time for the next wave of nausea.

"Can somebody get me some paper towels?" I called. "And a few plastic bags. And some latex gloves. And a lot of Lysol."

The room grew deathly quiet, and then everyone started talking at once. Most of the comments were along the lines of "Oh, gross!" A few people ran out of the room to either get supplies, Mrs. Shale, or perhaps fresh air. Mary walked up to Lauren, gripping her Coke so tightly I thought she'd crush the can between her fingers.

"You!" she yelled. "You did this! You put something in my cookie, Kate ate it, and now she's throwing up. You tried to poison me!"

Lauren's eyes flattened into angry slits. She walked up to Mary clenching her own drink. Without a word, she flung the soda in Mary's face.

Mary stood gaping for a moment. The liquid trickled off the ends of her hair and fell in brown streaks onto her costume.

Then she tossed her Coke all over Lauren. The next moment the two lunged at each other. Lauren grabbed Mary's hair and yanked her head downward. Mary plowed into Lauren's stomach and pushed her into the makeup counter. Bottles of foundation and tubes of mascara scattered everywhere. A bowl of Cheetos flew up in the air. For a moment they rained down like pieces of orange confetti. I took hold of Mary's arm, yelled "Stop it!" and tried to pull her off of Lauren. Jordan came around the other side and put his arms around Lauren so she couldn't make anymore flailing attempts to punch Mary. I pulled one way, Jordan tugged the opposite way, but neither girl let go of their grip on the other. Lauren had a hold on Mary's shoulder, and as Jordan yanked Lauren backward Mary's entire sleeve ripped off.

"Look what you've done!" Mary screamed. "You've ruined my costume! You've ruined everything!"

"We can fix it," I said, my breaths coming in rushes. "We can safety pin it back together." I didn't let go of Mary. Jordan didn't let go of Lauren. I could feel Coke soaking through my shirt from Mary's wet hair. "Are you done fighting?" I asked.

Mary jerked her arms away from me, then stood turning the ripped sleeve over and over in her hands. "Where am I going to find safety pins?"

Lauren shrugged off Jordan's grip and flung her wet hair away from her face. "I didn't put anything in your stupid cookie. Kate probably got sick from watching your pitiful performance." She ran her hand across her hair and looked down at the big brown spot on her dress. "Now I'm all sticky." Without another word she stormed out of the greenroom.

"I'll try to find safety pins," I told Mary. "Go wash the soda off your dress."

She nodded, then huffed out of the room, the sleeve still clutched in her hand.

I turned to the makeup counter hoping to see safety pins amongst the clutter and spilled bottles.

"I'll look in Mrs. Shale's office," Jordan said.

"Thanks," I called over to him. I sifted through a stack of Q-tips and bobby pins. Nothing.

Jordan opened the door, but before he left, he called my name. "Hey, Jessica. You know how you said one day I'd understand what you see in drama?"

"Yeah," I said.

"I'm still not seeing it."

Then he left.

I went through the entire makeup counter and everyone's coat pockets. I found paper clips, loose change, a battery, countless sticks of gum, and some things that would no doubt shock Tye's mother if she ever checked in his jacket. But no safety pins.

Some of the cast came back with cleaning supplies. Using an entire roll of paper towels—I mean, Kate is my best friend, but anybody's throw-up is way too yucky to touch—I cleaned up the mess. No one knew where Mrs. Shale had gone, although several people suggested it may have been into hiding. While Jeff helped me bag up the toxic waste, Jordan came back with a roll of duct tape. "It's the best I could find," he told me. "Can't she just wear another dress? How about the one you wear as Velma?"

See, that's really sweet. I mean, when a guy doesn't realize that a girl who's built like Pamela Anderson cannot just switch dresses with me—well, it says something good about him. "It wouldn't fit," I told him.

"Besides," Jeff said, "you're going to need it to play Anita.

I mean, you can't wear Kate's dress. She probably got vomit on it."

"I'm not playing Anita," I said. "We can't switch actresses midperformance. The audience will wonder why Velma is suddenly Maria's best friend."

Jeff pulled the ties on the garbage sack, then twisted them into a knot. "You have to play Anita. The play already stinks. What's going to happen if Kate starts heaving onstage?" He didn't give me a chance to answer. Holding the garbage sack away from him like it might try to reach out and grab him, he walked out of the greenroom.

"Maybe Kate is feeling better now," I said to no one in particular.

Jordan cocked his head and walked over to me. "Don't you want the part? I thought this was every understudy's dream. The agent is here, the reporters are here, then out from the lower ranks of the Jet rabble—a new star appears. You might actually be able to turn the play around. It's your chance at fame."

I screwed the Lysol lid back onto the bottle and put it on the makeup counter. "If Anita is suddenly a tall blond girl instead of a short brunette, it will make the play worse, not better. Besides, even if I felt horrible, I would drag myself out onstage and finish my part. Kate might not want me to take over now."

Jordan leaned up against the counter. "Ah yes, the show must go on. The show is all important. I forgot for a moment that you were one of those types of actresses." He smiled, but it was still an accusation. "The drama teacher screwed you over when it came to both trust and casting. The Marias are trying to claw each other to death—one of whom took the part you wanted, the other took your last boyfriend. What the principal didn't already rewrite, Andre is rewriting onstage. Your best friend is in the bathroom throwing up, and you're still trying to salvage this play."

Anyone else would have admired my dedication to putting on a good play. Unfortunately, I liked the one guy in the world who saw this as a character flaw. With palms up, I held my hands out to him. "What's wrong with that?"

"Drama is more important to you than anything else."

No, it isn't, I wanted to say, but we'd already had this conversation. He hadn't believed me then. I didn't know how to convince him now. "Jordan—" I started. I didn't get to finish.

Mrs. Shale bustled into the greenroom. "Jessica, put on a dress. You're now Anita." She ran one hand across her forehead, wiping away a sheen of sweat. "I guess I'll have to go out and explain to the audience that we've had an illness. Maybe it will garner some pity support for us." Her head swung around the greenroom. "Where are Lauren and Mary? Intermission is supposed to be over, and we can't do 'I Feel Pretty' without them."

"Is Kate going to be all right?" I asked.

"Her mother is taking her home. It's probably just a flu bug with bad timing."

Well, maybe. I didn't want to think Lauren was capable of poisoning someone, but it did make me wonder. I was surprised Mary wasn't here at Mrs. Shale's side pointing this fact out.

Mrs. Shale did a full turn of the room, then threw her hands up in the air. "WHERE ARE LAUREN AND MARY?"

"Probably washing Coke out of their hair," Jordan said.

Mrs. Shale swore—something that teachers are not supposed to do in front of students but that Mrs. Shale was making a production-night tradition of—then she walked to the door.

Jordan said, "Hey, you might need this," and threw the tape at her.

She looked at it blankly. "Why do I need tape?"

"Mary had a wardrobe malfunction. We couldn't find safety pins."

Mrs. Shale swore again, and gripped the tape. "I'll take care of her costume. Jordan, you go tell the audience that Anita is ill, and we'll be another couple of minutes. Make it sound bad. We need all the sympathy we can get."

Mrs. Shale left. Jordan left. I went to put on a dress. Five minutes later I stood in the wings repeating all of Anita's lines in my head. Jordan had told me I could turn this play around. I wasn't sure about that, but I was going to try.

The curtain opened to reveal the inside of Maria's bedroom. Maria was supposed to be dressing up to run away with Tony while her friends visited. But instead of looking like she was on her way to paint the town, Mary looked like she'd been hosed off in a barroom brawl. Wet hair clung to her neck in strands. She'd tried to wash out the big brown Coke spot on her white dress but had just managed to get her entire front damp.

When Lauren, similarly attired like a beached mermaid, asked Maria where she was going, and then said, "She's just dolling up for us," the audience laughed.

Mary's face turned bright red, and she forgot her next line. Lauren, who knew Maria's lines as well as Mary knew them, didn't offer any help. She just stood on stage, one eyebrow raised, a catlike smile plastered on her face.

After a few more moments of silence and glaring, the

orchestra struck up the music for "I Feel Pretty." This might have smoothed over the rough spot, except that while Mary danced and sang, her sleeve came unattached. It slid down her arm, and with one quick move, Mary flung the sleeve across the stage, and it hit Lauren in the face. Lauren stopped mid–dance step, picked up the sleeve, and tossed it back in Mary's face. Still singing, Mary grabbed the sleeve, walked over to Lauren, and tried to shove it down the front of her dress. Lauren grabbed Mary's arm, and then the two of them wrestled, twisting on the stage in an arm-locked position while Annabelle stood stiffly dancing in the background and picked up the last chorus by herself. *"I feel stunning, and entrancing, feel like running and dancing for joy . . ."*

Tye, who was to come onstage next, stood beside me with his mouth hanging open. I took hold of his arm. "Chino, go out there and break them up," I whispered.

He gave me an incredulous what-am-I-supposed-to-do look, but I just pushed him onstage. "Maria?" he called.

She was supposed to say, "I'm in here. I was just getting ready to—"

But neither Lauren nor Mary looked at him. They were too busy trying to push each other over and getting dangerously close to ramming into the set. Tye motioned to Annabelle to help him, and the two of them managed to pull Mary and Lauren apart. "So Maria," Tye called out when he'd heaved Mary away from Lauren.

She still didn't say her line—which was too bad, since it would have been quite clear to the audience that what she was getting ready to do was strangle her backup singer. Tye, bereft of any of his cues, just stared out at the audience, gulped, then spit out, "About that rumble you didn't think was going to happen—so it turns out Tony killed your brother."

Lauren and Annabelle were supposed to be offstage when Tye revealed this information because Jordan was about to come through the bedroom window to comfort Mary. Now all of the characters looked at one another as though not sure what to do next. "I guess we'd better go," Annabelle said, and tugged at Lauren's arm.

Lauren pulled her arm away from Annabelle and brushed her hair away from her face. "Witch!" she yelled at Mary, and then added, "Your brother deserved to die!"

Uh, nice attempt at an ad-lib save, Lauren.

"I'll show you who deserves to die!" Mary screamed back. "You'll die if you ever come near me again." Panting, she turned back to Tye. "What are you still doing here?"

He was supposed to search behind the furniture, grab the gun, and leave, but he just backed away from Mary with his hands raised until he had backed himself offstage.

Which was going to make it hard for him to shoot Tony in the last scene.

When he walked by me, I took hold of his sleeve. "The gun!" I whispered.

"Crap!" he said, and it wasn't a whisper.

Tye turned around and ran back onstage. Unfortunately, Jordan had just climbed through the window and now held Mary's grief-stricken form in his embrace.

Jordan and Tye stared at each other in horrified awkwardness. "I came back to get my gun," Tye said.

Another moment of silence filled the stage. None of them seemed to know how to handle this new plot twist. Finally Mary stood up and flung her arms outward. "Chino, don't shoot!" she yelled.

"I can't shoot. I don't have the gun," Tye said. Then he waved a finger at Jordan. "But as soon as I find it, I'm going to kill you, Tony." He rifled around behind the furniture, probably stalling for time.

Jordan and Mary stared at one another. They still had their last touching love scene and the song "There's a Place for Us" left to do. He wasn't supposed to leave yet, but it seemed a bit odd for him to stand there waiting for his killer to find the gun.

Offstage, Andre stood besides me with a handful of Cheetos, shaking his head. The last Cheetos I'd seen had been all over the greenroom floor, and I had the feeling that's where he'd retrieved this midscene snack from, but I didn't ask. I turned back to the stage, riveted, as though watching a train wreck.

"This is awful," I said.

Andre popped a Cheeto into his mouth. "I vote Chino kills Tony now and just puts the rest of us out of our suffering."

"He can't do that," I said.

"I'll do it. Do you want me to go onstage, grab the gun, and knock off all of them?"

"You can't shoot Tony. He's your best friend," I said. "And besides, you died two scenes ago."

Andre shrugged. "I'll get the rest of the gang members then. We'll hold the last shoot-out in Maria's bedroom. It will work."

"Yeah, because gang members frequently rumble in the middle of people's bedrooms."

Tye continued to search for the gun amongst the furniture, while Mary followed him around the stage wailing, "No, Chino! Go away! You can't shoot Tony *now*. I won't let you."

Like what—she expected him to say, "All right, then. I'll go, but I'll be back for the gun later. Please leave it out where it will be handy for me to pick up."

It was clear none of them knew what to do. Chino had to

get the gun, and yet he couldn't get the gun, because if he did, he wouldn't have a reason not to shoot Tony right then.

If Jordan had more experience with ad-libing, he might have been able to come up with something, but he stood frozen on the stage. He stared at neither Mary nor Tye but out into the audience—out at his father.

twelve

I took a deep breath, and then before I could think about all of the reasons it's unwise to insert yourself into a scene that your character doesn't belong in, I walked across the stage until I came to the others. "Maria, what's going on in here?" I demanded.

"Chino is trying to find Bernardo's gun to kill Tony," she gasped out.

"It will not do him any good," I said. "Bernardo told me that the gun has no bullets."

"In that case, I've found the gun," Tye said. He picked up the weapon and waved it around menacingly. "I'll go get bullets, and when I do, I will find you, Tony." He ran happily off-stage. Unfortunately, he exited through Maria's closet, which in real life would not have led out of the room, but none of us pointed that out.

I wasn't supposed to be here until the third scene, and now I'd have to think of some reason to leave and come back, then ad-lib the lines where I was shocked to find out Tony had been here.

It sort of made me wish I'd taken Andre up on his suggestion to shoot everyone.

The spotlight shone white all around me, making me

acutely aware of my unscripted presence on stage. I had to leave because . . . um . . . well . . . nothing came to mind. "I must go now," I finally said. "I'll be back later to talk to you, Maria, about *this boy*." I said the last part disdainfully, so it would be clear to the audience I wasn't happy to find the guy who'd stabbed my boyfriend in my friend's bedroom.

Jordan took hold of my arm as I walked by. "You saved us just now. I owe you my gratitude."

I knew he was talking about the scene, not his life, and it seemed ironic that he should mention this now. This was the guy who'd just criticized my dedication to drama. I took a step away from him. "You may owe me gratitude, but you won't ever try to pay the debt. It doesn't really matter to you." Which is something Anita might have told Tony, so I didn't feel bad saying it onstage.

From beside Jordan, Mary laughed nervously. She had no idea where I was going with this. I wasn't sure myself, but I didn't exit the stage just yet. Putting my hand on my hip, I tilted my head at Jordan. "You talk about people forgiving each other and getting along, but that only applies to others, not to you. You don't have any forgiveness in your heart, do you?" Which was also something Anita might say.

Real surprise registered on his face. I could see the struggle within him, trying to answer my accusation and trying to stay in part. "It's not a matter of forgiveness. It's a matter of priorities," he said. "Some people care about people. Some people only care about getting what they want from other people. Which are you?"

I took a step toward him. "I care about people. I care about you." Then in an attempt to stay in character, I added, "Um, *Maria*."

"Prove it," Jordan said.

I looked at Jordan. I couldn't see the audience, the agent, the cameras, the set, or even Mary nervously clenching her fists in the middle of the stage. Somehow all of that didn't matter right now. I only saw Jordan waiting for my answer.

I did care about him more than this play or any chance of fame it might offer.

Walking the rest of the way to him, I wrapped my arms around his neck and kissed him. Amazingly, he enveloped me in an embrace and kissed me back.

Okay, technically this was not something Anita would do. This was also not something Tony would do, especially since he was about to sing a love song with Maria. The audience was not going to get all weepy and emotional about their doomed love when he'd just kissed Maria's best friend in front of her.

I knew as I stood there kissing Jordan that I had ruined the play. Still, I kissed him. When I finally stepped away from him, he flashed a huge grin at me and squeezed my hand.

"Well . . ." he said. "Thank you for that demonstration of forgiveness. That was very charitable of you, you know, considering I just killed your boyfriend and all."

He glanced over at Maria. With her arms folded tightly against her chest, she glared darts of anger at us.

"I'd better go now." I smiled at Jordan one last time. I couldn't help myself. Then I hurried offstage.

From that moment on, well, let's just say the play reached the point of no return. Mary and Jordan sang their love song, but she sang all of her lines like she was mad, and the audience kept laughing. They also laughed when I came back onstage and sang my duet with Maria about how much she loved Tony. I sounded like some sort of trampy hypocrite, and she just sounded stupid.

It was a relief, really, when we'd plodded through the rest of act two and Chino finally shot Tony. The gang members acted entirely too happy about the event, and even Maria couldn't muster much despair at his passing.

When the curtain fell, there was a smattering of polite applause throughout the auditorium. Probably people clapping because they finally got to go home.

Traditionally, after every play the cast members went out into the front hallway to thank people for coming, receive flowers from friends, and pose for photo ops.

I didn't want to go, but Jordan dragged me out. Well, okay, he didn't actually *drag* me out, he just held my hand, and I wasn't about to let go of him.

"You were great," he told me as we walked.

"I ruined the play," I answered.

"That's why you were great. I'll always remember you ruined the play for me."

I squeezed his hand. "You acted so powerfully. The agent would have really been impressed if, you know, the rest of the play hadn't stunk."

He grinned back at me. "I didn't want to follow in my father's footsteps anyway."

Out in the hallway we saw Mrs. Shale sweating in front of a cameraman while a nearby reporter interviewed her.

"That was certainly the most unusual rendition of *West Side Story* I've ever seen," the reporter said. "I don't remember Maria wrestling with anyone or Anita throwing herself at Tony. Was that a surprise to you?"

Mrs. Shale twisted her hands together like she was wringing blood from her fingertips. "Live theater is full of surprises. That's why it's called performance art."

Jordan and I walked past her to where his father, mother, and the agent waited.

The agent spoke first. He shook Jordan's hand while the words shot out of his mouth. "Great performance. You showed a lot of creativity, kid. We'll have to get together for lunch sometime when you're visiting your old man in L.A." He released Jordan's hand and smacked Mr. Hunter on the back. "Well, I've got to run. Got some things to take care of back at the hotel. Thanks for inviting me to the show. It was great."

We all watched him walk away.

When he was out of earshot, Jordan said, "He hated it, didn't he?"

"Pretty much, yeah." Mr. Hunter laid one hand on Jordan's shoulder. "Don't take it so hard. Everybody has bad nights. You can't get down on yourself just because of one bad performance or one bad review—not that I'm saying this play will receive a bad review . . ." He glanced at his ex-wife, then back at Jordan. "Well, okay, actually I *am* saying that. Anyone who reviews this performance will kick it so hard they'll leave their footprints on it. And we'll just have to hope the people on *Extra* are too busy reporting Paris Hilton's latest scandal to show any clips of you kissing the wrong character. But the point I'm trying to make is that nothing is unfixable in Hollywood."

Jordan's mother leaned toward him. "I thought you did a fine job, dear."

"Thanks, Mom," Jordan said.

"I have other contacts in Hollywood," his dad said.

Jordan's mother smiled in that dreamy way parents smile when you're blowing out your birthday candles. "You reminded me so much of your father up there. It was just like watching some of his early stuff."

Mr. Hunter crossed his arms. "Is that supposed to be a compliment?"

Ms. Hunter dragged her gaze away from Jordan and patted her ex-husband's arm. "Of course it is." Now she turned the birthday-candle smile back at Jordan. "You know your father didn't start out getting top billing. At first he was a little shy and nervous about the whole thing, but once he'd been onstage a few times—well, he created magic. Directors had to give him the main part because otherwise whatever character he played just became the main part. He always stole the show." She gave Jordan another smile. "So don't be hard on yourself after your first performance."

Jordan dropped my hand and slid his arm around my waist. "It's okay, Mom. I don't want to be an actor. I just did this for fun. I'm only sorry it turned out so badly because the agent should have seen Jessica. She's really good."

Both of his parents looked at me for the first time.

"You did a fine job," his mother said.

I smiled back at her. "I ruined the play."

Now Mr. Hunter patted me sympathetically on the shoulder. "Yeah, but it was lousy even before your love scene with Jordan."

Ms. Hunter elbowed him. "Kit, this is one of those times when it's really okay to lie."

Mr. Hunter kept patting me on the shoulder. "You did a fine job."

"Thanks," I said.

He stopped patting my shoulder and slipped his hands into his pockets. For the first time I realized how close Jordan's parents were standing together. "So, do you still want to be an actress, even after tonight?" he asked me.

I hadn't realized Mr. Hunter had known this about me. Jordan must have told him. What else had he said to his father about me?

I glanced at Jordan, then back at his father. "Yeah, I think so."

"As tonight illustrated, sometimes it's a hard road to choose."

"I know."

"You have to make lots of sacrifices." Here Mr. Hunter stopped looking at me and glanced at his ex-wife instead. "Some sacrifices you make, and then wish you hadn't later."

I didn't know how to answer him, since he wasn't talking to me anymore; so I didn't say anything.

"And your family has to make sacrifices," he went on. "Maybe you never really appreciate how much they sacrifice so you can reach your dream. Maybe you forget to tell them thank you along the way. Maybe you forget to tell them I'm sorry."

Ms. Hunter reached over and squeezed his arm. "It's okay."

"It's not okay," he said. "And I'm sorry."

She leaned over and gave him a quick hug. For a moment they stood embracing in the hallway, and then they let go of each other and stared awkwardly at us.

"You want to go out and get something to eat?" Mr. Hunter asked.

"Sure," Jordan said. "As soon as we change out of our costumes."

I leaned against Jordan, liking the feel of his arm around me. "And we have to listen to Mrs. Shale's postperformance comments. Those might take a while tonight."

I was right about that prediction. She lectured us about everything. Even things that weren't our fault. I mean, we couldn't do anything about the fact that a near-fall into the orchestra pit threw off the percussion section.

Mrs. Shale dished out a fair share of the blame in my direction, but I didn't let it get to me. I couldn't get too worked up about our play when Jordan sat beside me holding my hand.

After calling my family to let them know I'd be in late, I went to IHOP with Jordan and his parents. It felt weirdly like a double date because Jordan's parents kept doing flirty things, like glancing over at one another, laughing, and in general ignoring us and talking to each other.

Jordan sent me a lot of I-told-you-so looks—which was ironic, since the last thing he'd told me about his parents was that they were doomed to live lonely, miserable lives.

On my doorstep later on that night, Jordan recounted the entire thing to me even though I'd been there while it happened.

"Did you hear how many times she called him Kit?"

"Yeah," I said.

"At least ten times."

"Yeah."

He took a step closer to me and put one hand against the door frame. "But I'm not getting my hopes up again. I mean, it's their lives. They have to decide how to live it."

"Right," I said.

"But did you see how he kept leaning over to talk to her?"

"He was the leaning tower of Hunter."

Then Jordan did some leaning himself. He bent down to kiss me, and I forgot all about his parents. In fact, I forgot about everything until the living room curtain momentarily swished open, spilling light out onto the doorstep.

Through the windowpane I heard Nicki's muffled voice talking on the telephone. "Well, it looks like Jordan is off the scam-market again." A pause and then, "Total make-out session happening on my front porch."

I banged on the window, and Nicki retreated to somewhere else in the house. Hopefully the darkness concealed my blushing. "Are you sure you want your parents to get back together? There's always the possibility you'll be saddled with a little sister, you know."

"I'll chance it." Jordan kissed me again on the top of the forehead. "See you tomorrow, Jessica."

And you know, right then I decided that I liked the name Jessica after all.

The next day Kate wasn't at school. At lunchtime I called her house, and her mom answered. Kate, it turned out, hadn't had the flu but appendicitis. She'd been rushed to the hospital last night but was now doing fine and resting after her surgery. I let Mrs. Shale and the rest of drama class know. I figured Lauren's name needed to be cleared, since Mary had publicly accused her of poisoning the gingerbread cookies.

Mary said a sullen, "Oh," as though disappointed Lauren hadn't been responsible, and then nothing else.

Everyone else murmured out sympathies.

After I sat down, Andre leaned over toward my desk, his usual smile gone. "I had my appendix out when I was ten. It hurt to breathe."

"She kept telling me she didn't feel well," I said, "but I didn't listen."

"And I gave her a bad time about all that political correctness stuff."

I tapped my pencil against my desk. "Maybe the cast should send her flowers."

He nodded. "I'll hit up the kids in class." Andre then went from desk to desk using his Riff-gangster accent to shake down everyone who had any money until Mrs. Shale finished marking the roll and told him to sit down. When he did, he had a fist full of cash.

Really, he wasn't a bad actor when he applied himself.

Jordan and I drove over to the hospital after school. His dad let him drive the Jaguar because his Civic was in the shop for a tune-up and a starter-motor check. Which was slightly awkward because my Civic was in the same shop getting the starter motor replaced. I was afraid Jordan's parents would see my Civic up on the racks and put two and two together, but according to Jordan, his mother had just shrugged and said, "Maybe your father's right about Hondas. They seem to have a rash of starter motor problems."

Jordan *so* lives a charmed life.

We spent a while talking with Kate, filling her in on what had happened in the performance until the nurse came in and yelled at us for making her laugh.

"Okay, no more talking about the play," I said after the nurse left. "We don't want Kate to rip her stitches. We'll have plenty of time to mock it later."

"Plus we have two more shows to put on," Jordan said cheerfully. "Who knows what will happen tonight. We might kill off more clarinet players than gang members."

Kate laughed again, and I swatted Jordan on the arm.

After a few more minutes of conversation, the nurse came back in and told us Kate needed to rest, so we strolled back to the parking lot and climbed into the Jaguar. I enjoyed riding in it today because I could sit back and relax as opposed to chewing all of my fingernails off.

I ran my hand over the seat with a sigh. "You're going to be sorry when your Civic gets out of the shop and you have to go back to driving it."

Jordan smiled. "I like my Civic. It has personality."

"Yeah, mine also has personality. Unfortunately, it's the personality of a psychotic prison inmate."

"I like your Civic too," Jordan said. "It brought us together."

I stopped running my hand over the soft leather interior long enough to consider this. "You have a point. Maybe I shouldn't call my car the Bratmobile anymore."

"You just have to be gentle with it," Jordan told me.

We drove back to the school to get ready for our next performance. Mrs. Shale had us all come in early to go over the rough spots. This involved a lot of glaring on her part and a solemn promise from the cast that we would not alter the script to the point that the play no longer resembled *West Side Story*. As it turned out, she didn't need to go through all the worry. The play went perfectly for the next two nights. No one forgot their lines, messed up their dance numbers, or died in ways other than prescribed in the script. In one way, it was a shame we hadn't been able to pull off a similar performance on the first night, when all of the cameras and the agent had come. But on the other hand, maybe Jordan and I would have never worked out things between us if the play had run smoothly that night. Or maybe Jordan's parents wouldn't have stopped fighting if they hadn't been so eager to make their son feel better about his mistakes. Maybe sometimes you need things to go rotten in order for things to go well. After all, timing is everything.